Editor: Talia Leduc

ISBN-13: 978-1998775347

Give feedback on the book at:
lorhainneeckhart@hotmail.com

Twitter: @LEckhart
Facebook: AuthorLorhainneEckhart

Printed in the U.S.A

Secrets

THE OUTSIDER SERIES

BOOK FOUR

LORHAINNE ECKHART

The Friessen Family Series Reading order:

The Outsider Series

The Forgotten Child (Brad and Emily)
A Baby And A Wedding
Fallen Hero (Andy, Jed, and Diana)
The Awakening (Andy and Laura)
Secrets (Jed and Diana)
Runaway (Andy and Laura)
Overdue
The Unexpected Storm (Neil and Candy)
The Wedding (Neil and Candy)

The Friessens: A New Beginning

The Deadline (Andy and Laura)
The Price to Love (Neil and Candy)
A Different Kind of Love (Brad and Emily)
A Vow of Love, A Friessen Family Christmas

The Friessens

The Reunion
The Bloodline (Andy & Laura)
The Promise (Diana & Jed)
The Business Plan (Neil & Candy)
The Decision (Brad & Emily)
First Love (Katy)
Family First
Leave the Light On
In the Moment
In the Family: A Friessen Family Christmas
In the Silence
In the Stars
In the Charm
Unexpected Consequences
It Was Always You
The First Time I Saw You
Welcome to My Arms
Welcome to Boston (A Paige & Morgan Short Story)
I'll Always Love You
Ground Rules
A Reason to Breathe
You Are My Everything
Anything For You
The Homecoming
When They Were Young (Link included FREE with The Homecoming)
Stay Away From My Daughter
The Bad Boy
A Place of Our Own
The Visitor
All About Devon
Long Past Dawn
How to Heal a Heart
Keep Me In Your Heart

The Friessen Family

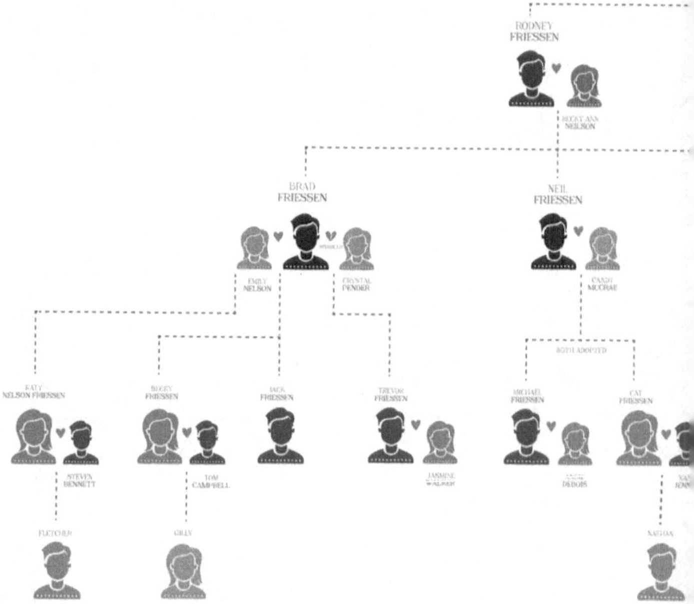

The Outsider Series

THE FORGOTTEN CHILD	BRAD & EMILY
A BABY AND A WEDDING	BRAD & EMILY &
FALLEN HERO	JED, DIANA & ANDY
THE SEARCH	JED, DIANA & ANDY
THE AWAKENING	ANDY & LAURA

The Outsider Series

SECRETS	DIANA & JED *with the entire Friessen Family*
RUNAWAY	ANDY & LAURA
OVERDUE	JED & DIANA
THE UNEXPECTED STORM	NEIL & CANDY
THE WEDDING	NEIL & CANDY *and the entire Friessen Family*

The Friessens: A New Beginning

THE DEADLINE	ANDY & LAUR
THE PRICE TO LOVE	NEIL & CANDY
A DIFFERENT KIND OF LOVE	BRAD & EMILY
A VOW OF LOVE	THE ENTIRE
A FRIESSEN FAMILY CHRISTMAS	FRIESSEN FAM

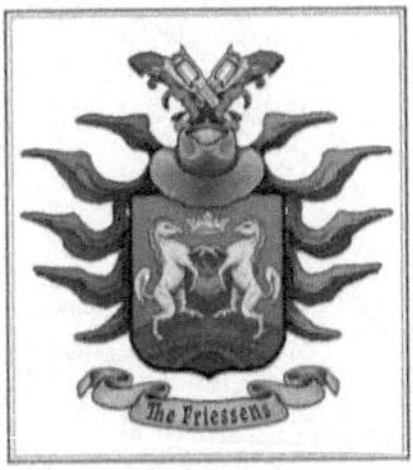

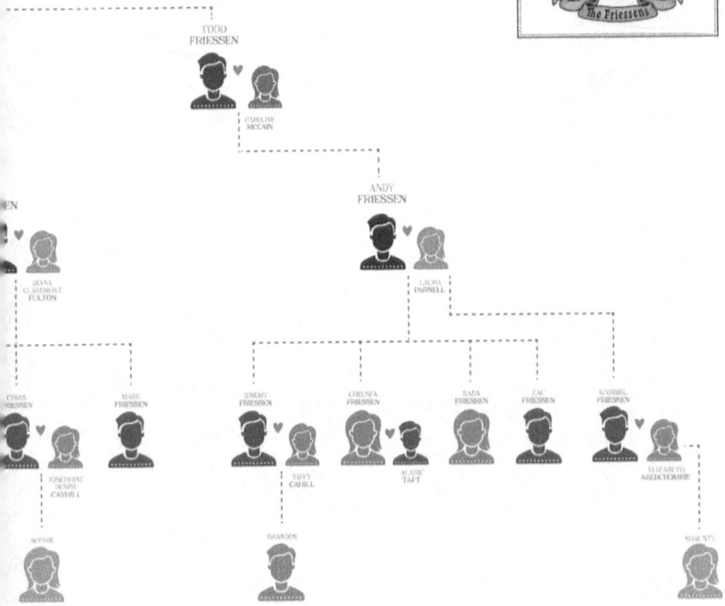

ens

HE ENTIRE FRIESSEN FAMILY
NDY & LAURA
ED & DIANA
EIL & CANDY
RAD & EMILY
ATY & STEVEN
ATY & STEVEN

The Friessens

LEAVE THE LIGHT ON	KATY & STEVEN
IN THE MOMENT	BECKY & TOM
IN THE FAMILY	THE ENTIRE FRIESSEN FAMILY
IN THE SILENCE	CAT & XANDER
IN THE STARS	DANNY & EVIE
IN THE CHARM	CHRIS & J.D.
UNEXPECTED CONSEQUENCES	CHRIS & J.D.

The Friessens

IT WAS ALWAYS YOU	KATY & STEVEN
THE FIRST TIME I SAW YOU	GABRIEL & ELIZABETH
WELCOME TO MY ARMS	CHELSEA & ALARIC
WELCOME TO BOSTON	PAIGE & MORGAN
I'LL ALWAYS LOVE YOU	JEREMY
GROUND RULES	JEREMY & TIFFY
A REASON TO BREATHE	TREVOR & JASMINE
YOU ARE MY EVERYTHING	MICHAEL & ANGIE
ANYTHING FOR YOU	
THE HOMECOMING	THE ENTIRE FRIESSEN FAMILY

Jed always told me he'd take care of everything. And I believed him, I trusted him, I love him.

—*"Wish there were truly men in the world like the Friessen Men." Reviewer Sara*

—*"This is an emotionally charged well written portrayal of a couple faced with a tragedy and the secrets that could destroy them." - Rita Herron, Author*

—*"The whole Friessen family show up in this story, and it was good to catch up with them all. The author really knows how to tug at your heart strings. Jed has a really tough time of it in this book, but I won't say more as I don't want to spoil the story." – Loves Reading*

—*" This was an excellent story, emotional and tragic, with a deeply heartfelt love story. – Melody*

In SECRETS, for Diana, Jed was the first man she trusted. He was the first man to show her what true love was. He was the father of her child, the one man she could always count on. Until one spring day Jed falls from the roof of the barn and Diana's world as she knows it begins to unravel.

Diana is forced to face two things, her husband's secrets, and what if... there was no Jed.

CHAPTER *One*

Jed Friessen slid back the covers and slipped out of bed, his bare feet hitting the cold wood floor and rousing him further from his restlessness. He'd tossed and turned most of the night, as he had the previous night, and the night before that. The clock now ticked two in the morning, and it was pitch black outside as he stood naked, resting his arm against the bedroom window, squinting at the shadowed outline of the barn and horse paddock. Every stall in the barn was full, six horses tucked in for the night. His eyes burned as he stared into darkness, and though he could see nothing amiss, he sensed an impending darkness that just didn't sit right. He raked his hand through his sleep-tousled brown wavy hair. It was on the longish side, and even his wife, Diana, had been nagging him to get a haircut, another thing to do—something else on his plate.

A horse nickered from the barn. Another answered softly in a way that said everything was fine. Maybe they knew he was watching, wondering; Jed could still feel that something wasn't right, and he didn't know exactly what it was. Maybe it was the worry plaguing his mind that wouldn't ease. It could also be the fact he'd been working day and night for months, readying this place for Echo Springs Equine Center, the official grand opening. It would be something different from just the trail rides and pack trips. This was for Diana and her need to help others. He'd struggled past every single hurdle tossed in his path, from overpriced lumber, to his grant being yanked, to cancelled horseback riding pack trips that dried up his income stream through the summer and fall.

It was a simple dream. Diana's dream. His wife, whom he loved more than his next breath. A horse facility specializing in bringing a special needs child together with a horse, because Diana believed, as did Jed, that allowing a child with special needs to learn skills through a connection with a horse provided a different advantage from your average therapy. It didn't replace the children's much-needed therapy, but it complimented and went hand in hand with it, centering the children, bringing balance into their life. And Jed would do anything to make sure his wife's dream came true.

Diana, his redheaded beauty and the mother of his ten-month-old baby boy, Danny, lay sleeping in the small double bed. She was the most stunning woman he'd ever met, a woman who had no idea how beautiful she was. And no idea how broke they were. The thing was, Jed was determined to provide for his family, on his terms, in his way, and only with his money, which wasn't much. After breaking his leg training that young squirrelly stallion, Jed had lost the spring and some of the early summer revenue from trail rides and pack trips. That money had always been enough to set him for the winter so he wasn't living hand to mouth, and it would have helped with some of the start-up costs.

Diana had a law degree and had tried to set up a law practice in North Lakewood, but the people still didn't give her the same trust they'd given some old white-haired fart. The only thing she'd managed to pick up, work wise, was a handful of wills and minor contracts, which amounted to squat. Besides, Jed made it clear to her that he wanted Danny raised at home by his mother, not stuffed into some daycare. They were a family, and he had no intention of seeing his wife in passing as she rushed off, working on some case that would drag her from him and Danny. It was selfish on his part, and he knew it, but he also knew Diana craved a family and deep roots more than her career.

Jed had bought this ranch outside North Lakewood a few years back at auction, and for a damn good price. But then he'd had to rebuild and fix just about everything in the house, the barn, and the three cabins he used for summer guests who booked horseback riding trips each year. He wasn't wealthy, but his family was. Jed was the only son to not take a plum dime from his father. Ever since he left home, he'd had no desire to take a handout, even though his father said it was his birthright. His two brothers, Brad and Neil, and his cousin, Andy, accepted the wealth handed to them in property and money. Jed didn't begrudge them for their easy lives, but he just didn't believe he could look himself squarely in a mirror and call himself a man if he was taking money from his family. A man stood on his own two feet, made his own way in this world, and that was how Jed chose to live his life.

Even as he struggled now, he couldn't bring himself to call his father for help, because to him that would be an admission that he had failed. So Jed had spent every spare minute turning over every rock to find the money to expand the barn, buy the extra tack, saddles, and horses, all at a bargain, thankfully. Except it had left him with nothing in his bank account and hours and hours of restless worry every night, and that was after the grant they'd been promised from the state had mysteriously disappeared. When he called the funding unit after getting the politically correct letter, they'd said funding had been cut for all areas for special needs. It was the economy, they said; but Jed learned that with governments, the first cuts always happened to the special needs, because they were the one sector of the population who didn't have the voice, the money and the time to fight back. They were and always would be an easy target. This knowledge also added to his irritation, like a sliver stuck under his nail so far that he couldn't get it out.

Jed hadn't told Diana about losing the grant. He knew she would have been crushed and would have insisted on picking up legal work, anything to help him out. Except the problem was Jed didn't believe a woman should ever support a man. That was his job, and as of late he wasn't doing so great. All they needed was cash, so as long as the students who'd signed up for the first classes next week all showed and paid in full for their six-week class, he'd have enough to pay the mortgage, buy feed for the horses and food for them. But they still needed to advertise, and there was the phone bill, medical insurance….

"Jed, what are you doing up?" Diana called out as she leaned on her elbow. The duvet slipped and exposed a hint of her creamy white breast as she sat up. She brushed back her long mussed hair with hands that brought him so much pleasure and blinked her tired, bright blue eyes. "Come back to bed."

Jed slid back under the covers and pulled her against him, running his hand down her slightly rounded belly.

Diana linked her finger with his. "Hmm, don't think I don't know you've had trouble sleeping." She rolled over and touched his cheek. "I don't need any light to see you're worried about something. What is it?"

"Go back to sleep. Just thought I heard something, is all." He brushed back her hair and kissed the tip of her nose.

"You're working too hard, but I think it's more than that. I don't need you to protect me. I need you to share what you're thinking, what you're worried about."

Jed rolled onto his back, rested his arm over his forehead, and sighed. Diana sometimes just wouldn't let things go. "It's fine, Diana. It's my job to look after you and protect you. What kind of husband would I be if I couldn't do that?" He realized too late he sounded sharp, abrupt, because next he knew, Diana sat up and slid her legs over the side of the bed.

"Diana… where are you going?" He reached over and grabbed her arm, feeling her tense up.

"Jed, I'm tired of you hiding things. And don't think I haven't noticed the stress this new horse center is putting on you. Is there something more I can do to help? What else has to be done? Maybe we should hire help."

Hire help! He couldn't believe she wanted to hire help. He ground his jaw, as that was the last thing they were going to do. "We don't need help. I'm almost done, just got to finish the roof, and then, when we start that first class next week, everything will be fine." And it would be, because the few who were interested and had signed up would be paying next week.

Diana slid around and rested her head on Jed's chest, and then her chin as she gazed up at him. "You're sure that's all?"

Jed rested his hand on the back of her head. "Next week everything will be fine. Let's get some sleep so we're not both tired tomorrow."

"I could help you get back to sleep." Diana slid her hand up his chest and drew circles with her fingernail around his nipple. She pressed a kiss into his navel, and then, trailing down, she pressed kisses lower until he pushed his head back into the pillow and felt himself sinking into a mind-blowing bliss that only Diana could give him.

She traced her fingers up his thigh and followed lower, tracing kisses to his knee and over to the other side. Jed sucked in a breath, drowning in his desire, and slid his own hands down her back, pulling her up and rolling her over onto her back.

Danny whimpered from his bedroom in their small two-bedroom home. Jed groaned. "Your timing sucks, Danny," he muttered.

Diana patted his arm to move him off her and started to get up.

"No, I'll get him" he said. "He may just need changing." Jed slid out of bed, the icy floor cooling his desire.

"Bring him back with you if he won't go back to sleep. We'll snuggle him between us. He loves that," Diana called out.

"Let's hope he goes back to sleep." Jed picked up Danny, who was now sitting in his crib, rubbing his tired eyes. "You're soaking wet." He kissed his head, his cheeks, and breathed in the fresh baby smell of his baby boy and changed him into a dry diaper and sleeper. Jed wrapped him in his blanket and sat in the rocker in the corner of the room, gently rocking him until he fell back asleep. And when Jed climbed back in bed, Diana too had fallen back to sleep. But not Jed, as he lay beside his wife, her warmth pressed against him, and he continued to worry he'd let his family down.

CHAPTER
Two

Jed lifted the thirty-two-foot extension ladder and carried it to the north wall of the barn. He leaned it against the unpainted wall and slid it open, locking the rungs, adjusting so it was level, touching the edge of the roof. He had two sheets of plywood left, and as he stared at the gaping hole of the open roof, he frowned. Would it be enough? It would be close, possibly uneven at the overhang. He glanced at the pile of shingles and at the roof again, and he knew he didn't have enough shingles, but then, half was better than none. A tarp would do for the other half for now.

Jed grabbed one sheet and slid it up the ladder ahead of him, lining it up over the beam. He hammered it in.

"Jed, do you want a sandwich?" Diana yelled from the ground. Danny was cooing in her arms.

"Sure, just give me half an hour. I got one piece of plywood left to get up here. Then I can start shingling." Jed swung his leg onto the ladder and stepped on the rung. The ladder slipped sideways, and Jed reached to grab hold of the roof edge, but his fingers seemed to brush over the plywood, and then he was falling backwards in the air. He heard a scream and felt everything go into slow motion. He felt nothing as he heard a whoosh, gazed up at a blue sky and puffy white clouds, and everything went black.

DIANA WATCHED in horror as Jed's ladder slid sideways. She jumped backward, clutching Danny to her side, and everything inside her froze—her breath, her sharp wit, and her legs felt cemented to the spot as Jed fell backwards and landed with a sickening thud on his back in the dirt. It took a second to realize Danny was screaming, and then she ran, dropping to the ground beside Jed.

"Jed!" she screamed. But he didn't answer, and then his eyes slid closed. Diana touched his head, then his chest. It rose up and down, but he lay there, unmoving and unresponsive.

Diana raced into the house, grabbed the phone, and dialed.

"Nine-one-one, what's your emergency?" a woman asked on the other end.

"My husband fell off the roof of the barn! He's not moving, I think he's unconscious!" Diana yelled into the phone. Danny was crying as he clutched her shirt. Diana struggled to hear the emergency operator, and every fiber, every muscle and bone inside her, trembled. She raced to the door with the cheap cordless phone, but it started to cut out, so she stepped back into the house and answered the woman's questions. "Yes, he's breathing. Just send an ambulance, and hurry. I need to get back to him. I can't stay on the phone." Diana rattled off the address and dumped the phone on the sofa as she ran back out to Jed.

He hadn't moved, and blood now trickled from the side of his mouth.

Diana wiped the blood with her hand as she clutched Danny to her, resting him on her hip. Jed's face was pale. He appeared asleep, but in a very different way that had a bone-chilling fear shredding her hard-won security, and launching Diana back into her childhood, when her shaky, unstable world was ripped away. Jed, the first man who taught her what love really was, her ruggedly strong alpha husband who was the first and only person who loved her deeply, protected her and fought her battles for her, lay motionless. It was a mere flash in that moment, terrifying her, a very real possibility of a life without Jed, and that was a living nightmare. She loved him so deeply. He was her husband, the father of her child and the first man she'd ever truly trusted. Diana touched his pale forehead, praying he'd respond, wince, yell, anything. "Jed, can you hear me, honey? Please answer me and tell me you're okay?" Her voice trembled.

He didn't moan or even blink. His breathing started to sound rough, like he was struggling with each breath. Something gurgled, and then blood dripped from the side of his mouth, again, in a long thin stream. A siren sounded in the distance. "Hurry up!" Diana screamed, as if that would get them there faster. "Hang on, Jed. Help is coming. Don't you dare die on me, or I will never forgive you!" she screamed at him again.

Dust and gravel spewed as the ambulance sped up the driveway. It was getting louder. Diana didn't want to leave Jed, but she had to get the paramedics, because they'd never see them where they were on this side of the barn. She ran, clutching Danny, who was still crying, to her side. She waved frantically as the ambulance pulled in and stopped in front of the house. Two paramedics jumped out.

"My husband's on the other side of the barn."

The paramedics followed Diana.

"He's unconscious. He won't answer me."

"Is he breathing?" a tall, dark-haired paramedic asked.

Jed hadn't moved as Diana raced around the corner. "Yes, but blood's coming out of his mouth now and he's having trouble breathing." Diana hovered over the two young paramedics, one dark-haired, one light-haired, as they knelt down on either side of Jed. "What's your husband's name?"

"Jed," Diana blurted out as she watched one paramedic shine a light in Jed's eyes. The other hooked him to an IV.

"Jed, can you hear me? If you do, I want you to squeeze my hand." The dark-haired paramedic held Jed's hand, then shook his head.

"What happened, ma'am?"

"My husband fell from the roof. He's putting a new roof on the barn." Diana pointed up. The paramedics both glanced up and then back at Jed.

"Did you move him, or is this how he landed?"

"He fell backwards. He landed on his back. I never moved him. Is he going to be okay?" Diana asked frantically, as Danny's tiny little fingers dug into her bra, as he continued to cry fretfully. She patted his back, kissed his head as her heart pounded long and loud, and each breath was a struggle, as if she'd just run a mile. She knew she needed to get Danny out of there, but she couldn't leave Jed. So she tried to hold Danny's head and turn him away so he couldn't see his daddy. "It's okay, baby." Diana bounced Danny on her hip to try to quiet him, kissing his face, his cheek as her gut knotted so tight she thought she'd go crazy.

"We need to move him. He may have punctured a lung. We're going to need to get a chest tube in him."

Diana touched her face. Her hand shook violently as she watched and listened to the paramedics. One of them raced back to the ambulance and returned with the stretcher and equipment, medical supplies. The other was on his radio, talking. They cut open Jed's shirt. Diana turned away to shield Danny from seeing them cut into Jed. When she turned around, they'd already put on a neck collar and had threaded a tube down her husband's throat. He was hooked up to a bag that the other paramedic squeezed for oxygen. There was blood on his side, more tubing and tape. What the hell were they doing to her husband? Then they eased him onto a backboard, strapped him down.

"Okay, let's get going," one of them shouted, and they wheeled the gurney to the ambulance and loaded Jed in.

Diana followed. "Which hospital are you taking him to?" she asked the light-haired paramedic before he closed the door.

"Cascade in Arlington, ma'am. They can assess from there whether to fly him out to a trauma center."

Danny was shaking in her arms, his eyes big and wide. Diana kissed his head, his face, and did her best to calm him, let alone herself. She raced inside the house, grabbed her purse and Danny's diaper bag, stuffing an extra sleeper, diapers and a jar of baby food inside, and raced out the front door to her SUV, keys jangling. She looked up at the cloud of dust, listening to the sirens wailing as she buckled Danny into his seat and he started to cry again. Diana stopped, placing her hand on his stomach. "Please, Danny, don't cry. Let Mommy drive, and we're going to follow

Daddy." Diana shut her eyes as Danny grabbed for her. She needed help.

She dug through her purse for the cell phone she rarely used, hoping it was still charged. She powered it on—the green bar showed that the battery was half charged. She shut Danny's door. He was still fussing as she hurried to the driver's side, dialing her phone. "Please answer," she whispered as she slid under her wheel, closed her door and started her SUV. She cranked the wheel sharply and sped down the long dirt and gravel driveway, and the call went right to voicemail, "It's Diana. Jed fell off the barn roof. He's hurt bad. The ambulance is taking him to Arlington. I'm heading there now. Please call me," she shouted into the phone. Danny was wailing from the back.

Diana tossed the disconnected phone on the passenger seat, and as she turned onto the highway, she pressed the gas, praying her husband would be okay.

CHAPTER *Three*

"Why won't anyone tell me what's going on! My husband was brought in by ambulance an hour ago. He fell off the barn roof," Diana rattled off frantically. Danny was now rubbing his eyes, still fussing.

The plump, dark-haired nurse behind the emergency room glass rustled through some papers and then said, "Excuse me, and I'll see if I can find out something for you."

Diana had been there an hour and had been told to wait. Apparently, a gunshot victim had been brought in and his friends had shown up, which brought extra security to the waiting area, where she'd been told to wait during the chaos by a security guard, an orderly, and another nurse.

"Diana!" Andy Friessen, Jed's cousin, called out to her. He strode toward her, weaving through the crowded waiting area. He was tall, dark haired, wearing blue jeans and a dark navy shirt, with Laura, his young blond bride, wearing a peach sundress, behind him. By the time he reached her, the nurse had returned with a young doctor in blue scrubs. Danny picked that moment to let out a howl and pushed at Diana's chest to try to get down.

"Danny, please, baby…"

"Diana, give him to me." Laura held out her slender arms, and Danny slid happily into them. She patted his back and rocked him in place.

"Your husband was the one brought in who fell from a roof?" The doctor had a medium build and had ruffled brown hair that was in desperate need of a haircut.

"Diana, what happened? Jed fell from where?" Andy interrupted.

Diana darted a glance between Andy and the doctor, feeling flustered, like a lost young woman unsure of whom to give her attention to. She jammed her hands in her long red hair, which was loose and falling from the ponytail she'd fastened this morning, and looked from one man to the other. "He fell from the barn roof. He just stepped onto the ladder and it tilted sideways. I couldn't do anything, I could only watch as he reached out and tried to grab the edge of the beam, but he couldn't get a hold of it, and he fell backwards, and… and he hit the ground so hard I swear it shook, and… I heard this echo. I hurried…. How is my husband?" Diana couldn't seem to form a sensible word, let alone a sentence that made any sense.

Both men watched her, and she didn't miss their concern. The doctor pressed his hand on Diana's shoulder, then glanced at Andy and then at Laura, who stood behind Andy, swaying side to side with Danny in her arms. The doctor gestured with his head, then guided Diana over to the side of the waiting room, away from all the people milling around. Andy and Laura followed. The nurse slipped away.

"Where is my husband?" Diana shouted. Andy reached out and rested his hand on her other shoulder. The doctor stepped back and glanced around, appearing irritated. Diana was shaking.

"Your husband has a skull fracture and two cracked vertebrae, and there is pressure on the spinal cord. Right this moment, your husband is being readied to be transported to Harborview, which is a level-one trauma center."

Diana blinked and then stuttered: "I don't understand. I want to see my husband."

The doctor glanced up at Andy and back to Diana. "Your husband is unconscious. We ran a CT, and there's significant brain trauma. He also punctured a lung in the fall. As soon as he's stable, he'll be airlifted."

"I want to see my husband," she demanded again.

The doctor shook his head. "I'm sorry. We need to get your husband ready—"

Andy cut him off quite abruptly. "Look, that's my cousin in there, and we need to see him. His wife needs to see him."

Just then, shouting and a scuffle started behind them as two hotheaded teens started shoving each other and uttering threats. Danny was crying again.

"Doctor, we need you back here," a nurse shouted, and the doctor started to turn away before saying to Andy, "Come on, I'll take you to him. But you *have* to stay out of the way."

Andy pulled Laura behind him and put his hand on Diana's back as they all followed the doctor down the corridor to a trauma room.

Andy turned to Laura and said, "Wait right here. Don't let Danny see."

She nodded. "Take Diana in. I'll try and calm him down, but he needs to not be here."

Diana pushed open the door, Andy right behind her. An intern and a nurse in scrubs were beside the bed. A monitor was hooked up, and Jed had a tube down his throat and was hooked up to a ventilator. His eyes were closed, and his face was pale. An icy cold numbness replaced all the warmth in Diana's body, and her hand trembled as she touched her mouth. "Jed?"

The nurse looked up and said with a warning, "Don't touch him. You can stand there and talk to him." Diana moved beside the bed. Tubes extended from Jed's arm. A bag hung beside the bed, and there was blood in it. He was in a neck collar, and he had dried blood from the side of his mouth, and his eyes were closed, just as before, as if he were asleep. But it was different, because she didn't think Jed slept much, and certainly not deeply. Every time she moved at night, he moved with her, whispered to her. Responded to her. She wanted him to open his eyes to reach for her and pull her into his arms and tell her it would be okay.

The door pushed open and the doctor said, "The chopper's here. We're moving him now."

Andy pulled Diana to the side as Jed was wheeled from the room. The same average-looking doctor put up his hand to stop them from following. "He's being flown to Harborview." The doctor stared up at Andy. "I can't let either of you go with him. The chopper's full, and we'll have him there in thirty minutes. You'll have to drive."

The doctor walked away, and Diana watched as her husband was wheeled onto the elevator and the doors slid closed. Her gut felt as though someone had sliced it open with a butcher knife. She couldn't bear to be without him.

Andy grabbed Diana's shoulder and turned her. Laura clutched a whimpering Danny, who was reaching for Diana. She knew he was terrified—hell, she was terrified.

"Diana, I'll drive you. Laura, take Danny home with you." Andy led both women through the emergency doors, into the parking lot. "Diana, where's your car?"

She stopped and turned in a circle in the crowded parking lot, blinking as she stared at the rows of cars and then tapped her forehead with her hand. "I can't remember where I parked."

Andy jogged past the rows and then shouted from two rows over, "Over here." Diana reached for Danny, who was still crying. His eyes were red and his nose was running. This wasn't good for him at all.

"Come on, Diana. Andy will get you there. It'll be okay," Laura said to Diana as both women hurried two rows over to Andy, where Diana's SUV was parked halfway down the row at a ridiculous angle, close to a black Mercedes, in a way that would make it difficult to get out.

"Where are your keys?" Andy took Danny from Diana, and she stuck her hand in her pocket and yanked out the keys. He quickly grabbed them, passing Danny, with his little pudgy hands waving frantically, back to Laura.

"I'm going to back it out. Laura, you and Diana stand out of the way." Andy crawled in the passenger side.

Laura grabbed her arm. "Diana, step back." She pulled her to the other side of a red pickup, and Andy carefully backed out her silver SUV and then left it running as he slid out.

Diana hurried to the back door and grabbed the diaper bag, passing it to Laura. "Are you okay with Danny?"

Laura was just twenty, and a very pretty young lady, but it was then, in a passing glance, that Diana noticed certain recent changes. Laura's once-long blond hair was now cut into a short bob, which emphasized her round, innocent face.

"Diana, I'll take him back home with me," she whispered as she took the diaper bag and hooked it over her other shoulder. "You go with Andy."

Andy strode closer to Laura, and Diana didn't miss the stilted awkwardness between the two of them, although maybe it was just her.

"Laura, take Diana's SUV. Diana, we're not moving the baby seat. I'll take you in my truck. Laura, tell Jules to help you. I'll call you later to make sure Danny's okay," Andy dictated to Laura, and again Diana noticed a tension between them. Andy took Danny from Laura as she stood awkwardly behind him while he buckled him in back. And then he grabbed Diana's hand as he led Laura to the driver's side. "Are you okay to drive?"

"I'm fine. I can do this. Just take Diana and call me later."

Andy hesitated a second and leaned down to kiss Laura. Even Diana realized there was no passion in that kiss. Geez, to her it seemed to have been done more out of duty. Laura blushed as she slid under the wheel and closed the door, and then she drove away. Andy still held Diana by the hand. "Let's go." He pulled her with him over one row, to where his large, dark blue truck was parked. He held the passenger door open and helped her in, went to his side and slid under the wheel. Diana's hand shook while she tried to fasten the seatbelt.

Andy moved her hand with a swipe of his and buckled her belt for her, and then he backed out and pulled to the exit behind Laura. Laura had turned left, heading toward the highway that would lead out to Andy's family's estate, where Andy and Laura still lived. Andy didn't give Laura a second glance as he turned the other way.

A chopper was lifting from the rooftop. Diane pressed her hand to the glass and watched as it lifted into the sky, the blades vibrating sharply through the air, pounding in rhythm with Diana's heart. She watched as it headed west toward Seattle. She couldn't look away, staring until it was just a speck in the distance. And Andy drove on with her in silence.

CHAPTER *Four*

"How did you know to come to the hospital?" Diana asked Andy after what felt like an hour of sitting in silence. After all, she'd called Rodney and Becky, Jed's parents, not Andy. Before Andy could answer, his cell phone rang.

"Hello."

Diana watched Andy, her hands fisted in the same tight grip as her stomach.

"I've got Diana. No, he's been airlifted to Harborview, in Seattle. He should be there now. They airlifted him from Arlington about an hour ago." Andy glanced over at Diana, then back at the road. Even with Andy's dark glasses, she could see the concern that tightened his face. She tried to relax her hands and then stared at the old dingy runners she'd put on this morning, her faded blue jeans with the tear in the knee, and she realized then she was wearing one of her older pink t-shirts splattered with orange, probably from Danny's carrots. She tried to wipe off the crusty stain, then picked at it with her short nails and gave up.

"As soon as we get there, I'll call you. We'll track down a doctor, find out what's going on. Good, good, glad he's on his way."

Diana leaned into the plush leather and watched Andy again, listening to the one-sided conversation as he continued to glance at her and then back to the road.

"No, Danny's with Laura. I had her take him back to our place. She'll have some help to look after him."

Diana jerked her head at Andy, wondering what he meant by that. She knew how dedicated a mother Laura was to Gabriel, the baby she'd had when she was sixteen and very much alone in the world.

"Okay, I'll see you soon." Andy stuffed his cell phone back in his shirt pocket. He signaled right and moved over a lane, taking the off ramp leaving the freeway. "That was Uncle Rodney. Their flight to Seattle leaves in an hour."

Diana nodded. She didn't have the energy to speak as a giant knot twisted up her stomach and her heart. Her eyes burned as if she'd been crying nonstop, but she hadn't shed a tear.

"We're almost there, Diana." Andy reached over and took her hand in his. "Jed's going to be fine. You know that. He's a big strong guy, and it takes a lot to bring one of us down—"

Diana pulled her hand away. "He shouldn't have been up there."

Diana stared straight ahead but could feel Andy's eyes on her. "What do you mean?"

"He's been worried, really worried. He hasn't been sleeping. I kept asking him what was wrong, but he kept saying everything was fine, always an excuse, as if to protect me. What is it with you Friessen men, needing to do everything yourself, your way? He needed to finish the roof on the barn. We're scheduled to open our riding center next week. I have five special needs kids booked. Last night I wanted him to hire help, but he nearly bit my head off, said he was almost done. I shouldn't have pushed so hard for this center. It's my fault he's been working so hard. He's never that careless. I watched from the ground.... I asked him if I could make him a sandwich. I was worried and just wanted him to take a break, to take it easy for a minute, and he stepped onto that ladder and it slid away from the barn just like that, so easy, and he fell backwards. He hit the ground so hard it shook. And he never moved. He said nothing. And I could only watch." She rattled on and finally gasped.

"Diana, don't blame yourself. It's not your fault."

"Andy, you never answered me about how you knew to come to the hospital." Diana looked at the floor and beside her. "Oh no, I forgot my purse in my SUV. My cell phone's there, too."

"Diana, stop worrying. Listen, Uncle Rodney called me right after he got your message. Laura and I were already in town."

She had to change the subject, or she thought she'd go insane. "What's going on with you and Laura, Andy?"

He darted a quick glance at Diana—a glance she was positive was laced with irritation before he quickly masked it. "Everything's fine with me and Laura. It's just that she's so young."

The way he said it made her wonder if it was regret. "You didn't have to marry her, Andy. There is a big difference between feeling love and feeling responsibility."

"Just drop it, Diana. You have my cousin to think of," he snapped.

The way he said it was like a splash of icy water in her face. "You can be so cruel sometimes, Andy." She turned away, looking out the window at the bustling city.

"I'm sorry, Diana. I just don't… I don't want to burden you with my problems." He let out a heavy sigh.

"Andy, do me a favor. Distract me, please, because right now my head and my thoughts are going to some pretty dark places where I don't want to go." She gasped, and this time her eyes burned with unshed tears and she had to fight to hold them back.

"I felt responsible for Laura when she lived in her car because she couldn't pay rent, because Mother fired her during one of her temper tantrums. I was supposed to help her find a job, but I got distracted. And you know all this because you were there, Diana, when the sheriff took Gabriel and shoved him in foster care, a home that kept him locked up. I didn't see any other answer than to marry her. She's attractive, and sexually—"

"Oh, whoa, way too much detail, Andy. I don't need to know about your sex life." Diana felt her face heat when she pictured Andy in bed with Laura.

Andy chuckled, and Diana glanced over at him.

"Andy, don't break her heart. She doesn't deserve that, either. By the way, how's Gabriel?" She watched him closely as he drove.

"He's doing good, a quiet boy. Had him in for tests to find out why a four-year-old doesn't talk. I've got one of the best pediatricians in the state looking after him. I know Laura was relieved when Doctor Anderson said he was ruling out autism. He suspects it's some type of auditory processing disorder."

"Wasn't Laura told by some guy at a free clinic that he was just delayed?"

"Yeah, well, let's not go there. I told this pediatrician that and he frowned, shook his head and said most doctors don't have the skill to differentiate, let alone diagnose, a special needs child. So instead of referring the child to a specialist, they say he's just *delayed*. It's about time, and money, and politics. But Gabriel's getting help. I hired someone to come and work with him, got him out of daycare permanently. Laura doesn't need to work, so she can spend time helping Gabriel." Andy waved his hand in the air as if he'd decided what everyone was to do for Gabriel, including Laura.

"I admire your dedication to a child that's not yours, Andy. But do you mind if I give you a little advice?" She slid her bum around on the leather seat.

Andy didn't respond, and she didn't miss the slight twitch in his cheek.

"She's vulnerable, innocent, and you're dictating to her. For God's sake, you can't tell her what to do, sleep with her and not give yourself to her. You're married. You either build a relationship together—"

"Or what, Diana? For God's sake, open your eyes, woman. Jed does the same thing to you. Weren't you just saying he's hiding something from you? In case you're not seeing it, he's telling you what to do, as well. You're a lawyer, Diana. Where're all your clients? Why aren't you practicing law?" He didn't give her a chance to answer. "You're at home, having Jed's baby right where he wants you, under his thumb, so he can control you."

Diana leaned against the door, staring in disbelief at the man beside her. "Andy, you've got a mean streak in you, and it comes out when your back's against the wall. You've got it all wrong. I love Jed. He loves me and Danny, and he'd walk barefoot into hell for me, and I know that. You know the difference between how you treat Laura and how Jed is with me?"

Andy pulled into the hospital parking lot and into the first available spot. He turned off the engine and faced Diana.

"Jed respects me." Diana yanked open her door and slid out, shoving it closed. Andy glanced at her as she shuffled beside a gray car in the parking spot beside him.

"I'd walk barefoot through hell for you, too," he whispered as he yanked open his door and stepped down from his truck.

CHAPTER Five

Diana forgot her irritation with Andy as they started toward the main door of Harborview Hospital. She practically jogged to keep up with him. He pulled open the front door for her and waved her in, and she didn't miss the distant, odd look in his eyes before he glanced away. He didn't touch her back, her shoulder, or try to take her hand, as he'd done earlier. He walked straight to the information desk, and Diana followed and stood beside him when he asked the woman with short jet-black hair about Jed Friessen.

"Diana." It was a deep male voice that called out.

She turned and saw Brad, Jed's brother, walking toward her, wearing faded blue jeans, cowboy boots, and a jean jacket, with a fairly new tan cowboy hat on his head. He had the same powerful build as Jed—the same heavy stride. Damn good-looking, but then, all the Friessen men were.

"Brad, you're here. Did you see Jed?" She ran toward him.

Andy was all of sudden beside her, too, reaching out and patting Brad's arm. "Rodney called you?"

Brad spoke over her head to Andy. "Dad called as soon as they got Diana's message. I grabbed a ride on a float-plane heading to Seattle as soon as I heard they were moving Jed. I got here right after he arrived."

It took Diana a minute before she realized Brad was watching her with deep brown eyes, a shade darker than Jed's. He rested his large hand on her shoulder and squeezed before pulling her into his arms. She rested her head against his chest but felt stiff as a board.

He stepped back and looked down at her, his face an image of concern. "Diana, are you okay, honey?"

"You didn't answer me about Jed. Where is he?" Her voice sounded pathetic even to her own ears.

Brad glanced over her head, again at Andy, and that set her blood to boil.

"What the *hell* is wrong with you Friessen men? I'm not some mindless twit, and when you don't answer, I'm thinking the worst, that something has happened to my husband…."

"Hey there, Diana." Brad kept his hand on her shoulder, holding her as though she was his responsibility and he expected her to fall apart. "Come over here and sit down." He tried to lead her to the lobby, where the sofas and chairs were, but Diana stopped after a few steps and smacked his hand away.

"Brad, for God's sake, please. Where's my husband?"

He wrapped his arm around her shoulder and moved her toward the sofa. "Diana, I want to talk to you about Jed. Sit down, honey."

Diana finally relented when she noticed people staring at her in the lobby. She was causing a scene. Brad sat right beside her. Andy stood in front of her, his arms crossed.

"Jed's upstairs in ICU. They need to take him into surgery. There is pressure on his spine. He broke it in two places, and they need to put in a screw."

"Oh God, Brad."

"Diana, they're most concerned with the head trauma. He has a skull fracture, and there is a bone fragment pressing on his brain. They have to go in and relieve the pressure." Brad never took his eyes off her. He was Jed's older brother, a man she didn't know very well, but Jed idolized him, always had. Brad now owned the family ranch outside Hoquiam, where Jed grew up, with new wife, Emily, his autistic son, Trevor, Emily's little girl Katy from her first marriage, and their new baby, Becky. What she did know about the Friessen men was that they were all about family.

"I want to see my husband." She said it again because she needed to see him—to touch him—and until she saw him, this gigantic ache in her chest wouldn't ease.

Brad glanced up again at Andy, who nodded. "Okay, let's go up."

CHAPTER
Six

The elevator doors slid closed, and Brad pressed a button. An elderly woman hunched over with a cane was also in the elevator. Andy hesitated and didn't get on, but he said he'd call Rodney and give him an update. Again, Diana wasn't consulted.

She could feel Brad's heat, his energy, beside her. He was definitely not a man who took orders from anyone. The elevator dinged, and the door opened. Brad pressed his hand into Diana's back. "This is it, this way." He guided her down to the nurse's station, where doctors, nurses, and other hospital personnel bustled.

"Doctor Hardy," Brad called out.

A tall man in light blue scrubs, with a solid, heavy build, like someone who worked out in a gym, was scribbling something on a chart. He glanced up.

"This is Diana, Jed's wife. She just got here." Brad's large hand rested against Diana's lower back.

The doctor clicked a pen and popped it in his pocket, then handed the chart to another man as he issued orders about some tests Diana had never heard of before. When he glanced down at Diana, he pushed away from the high counter. He had short gray hair and light blue eyes, and he gave Diana all his attention. "Mrs. Friessen—"

She held up her hand. "Diana… Please, call me Diana." She realized too late that her response sounded quite sharp. "Sorry."

"Diana, we need to get your husband into surgery sooner rather than later. As I explained to your brother-in-law here, the fall fractured his spine in two places. Anita, can you hand me the chart for Jed Friessen?" A short, blond woman handed a chart to the doctor. He flipped it open and yanked out what looked like an x-ray. "Right here and here." He slid his finger over a white spot on the spine, and Diana stared at what she assumed were two lines showing the spinal fractures. "We need to get in now and relieve pressure at the earliest for the best outcome, but the primary concern is the skull fracture. When your husband fell, he suffered what is called a depressed skull fracture." He pulled out another film from the chart and held it up, showing the image of a skull, but this time she could see the cloudy spot he spoke of that was pressing into the brain. "We need to get in and relieve the pressure now."

Diana nodded, wondering why she couldn't pull it together. "When can I see my husband?"

The doctor hesitated only a second when he looked at Brad, then reached out and touched Diana's shoulder. "Come with me." He walked her to the end of the corridor. Every room had a glass wall so visitors could see inside, and a patient was in each bed. The door swished open, and the doctor walked Diana in to where Jed lay in a hospital bed, a tube down his throat. One machine was pumping air, another beeping. Fluid bags were hanging, tubes in his arm. To Diana, it looked overwhelming, as if he were hooked up to everything, and what she saw was his too-long wavy brown hair sticking out everywhere, as if he hadn't brushed it in a week. Diana started to hurry to his side to grab his hand, but the doctor stopped her and said, "You can hold his hand, but don't try to hug him or move him." He said it in a way that she took as informative and not overbearing, as both Brad and Andy had been with her.

Diana glanced up at the distinguished-looking doctor and then slid her shaky hand under her husband's limp one. For a moment, she willed him to squeeze hers as he always did. She skimmed his large, dry palm, which normally swallowed her hand. She traced the calluses on his hand and then squeezed, again hoping he'd squeeze hers back. But nothing happened. He lay there, unmoving, his eyes closed, and it was the loneliest feeling Diana had ever experienced.

"Did he open his eyes at all?"

"Your husband has not regained consciousness. Take a minute with him. The nurse will be in shortly, and we'll need your signature on the consent."

Diana stared at Jed, her strong, overprotective husband, lying there helpless. The door slid open, Brad touched her arm, and she glanced up at him.

"Diana, I'll be right back. I just want to talk to the doc." She knew Brad was worried about her and trying to protect her. She got that. It was different from Andy, because what she sensed with Brad was an unspoken understanding he had with Jed to look after her. She watched Brad outside the room with the doctor, and Andy strode up and joined them. He shook the doctor's hand. His dark glasses were gone, but there was something in his eyes, the way he glanced through the glass at Diana as the doctor talked, that had her stepping closer to the bed—

closer to Jed. She glanced down at Jed, swallowing. The door swished open, and she glanced up at Brad. Andy waited outside the room, speaking with a floor nurse, his back to Diana.

"What did you say to the doctor?" Diana touched the back of Jed's hand. The glass door slid open, and a nurse walked in and checked his IV bag. When Brad didn't answer, Diana looked up at him.

"Jed's always done things his way." His expression softened, and he winced. "Sorry, I asked the doc to give me best and worst case scenarios for Jed from the fall he took."

"And what did the doctor say? Is my husband going to wake up? Will he be paralyzed? I need to know, Brad." Diana watched Brad as he winced and dropped his gaze.

He put his arm around her and said, "He said to get him in surgery before he'll give a prognosis, and the first twenty-four hours are critical."

"Mrs. Friessen," a nurse with a clipboard strode in, "I need you to sign the consent, and we really need to get your husband prepped for surgery now."

Diana accepted the clipboard. She read over the legalese, which should have come naturally, but every sentence was a jumbled mess she could make no sense out of. "For God's sake, I'm a lawyer, Brad. This should be easy…."

Brad squeezed her shoulder. "Diana, it's okay." He leaned closer, reading the release with her, and then handed her the ballpoint pen. "Diana, sign it."

Their eyes locked, and she nodded because she trusted Brad. She clicked the pen and scribbled her name.

The nurse reappeared and took the clipboard. "We need to get him ready. There's a waiting room around the corner. Someone will be down to let you know when we take him in."

"Can't I stay with him, please? I won't get in the way," Diana pleaded.

The nurse bustled around the bed and set the chart on the side table as she checked his IV tubing. "No, I'm sorry. We need to get him ready."

Diana wasn't ready to leave him. She wanted—needed—more time with her husband. She took his hand in both of hers and stroked the tanned, freckled skin on the back of his hand, and she leaned over and kissed his cheek, willing him again to respond to her. But he didn't.

It was Brad who touched her shoulder, slid his hand down her arm. "Diana, come on, honey."

She stepped back and studied every inch of Jed in a faded blue hospital gown, covered with a sheet to his waist, hooked up to tubing, filling every inch of that hospital bed.

Brad led her out, his arm loosely around her shoulder, to the waiting room, where Andy was leaning against the window ledge, one booted foot crossed over the other.

"They're getting him ready for surgery. Did you call Dad?" Brad asked.

Andy nodded. "They're on their way." He glanced at Diana. "I called Laura. Danny's fine. I sent one of the ranch hands over to your place to look after things, feed and water the horses."

Diana said, "I forgot, I'm sorry.... I forgot about the horses. Oh, God. And Danny, he's never been away from me." She pulled her dingy t-shirt from her full breasts, pinching her bra. "I'm still nursing him."

"I'll go and get him. I didn't realize." Andy brushed her arm and looked down at her with tenderness before snapping his gaze back to Brad.

Diana felt Brad press his hand tighter, as if holding her closer.

"Mom will be here soon. She'll help with Danny," Brad

said. The Friessen men were all tall and handsome, each of them with a body every woman dreamed would hold her at night. But it was Jed she pictured, lying helpless in that bed, the one man who took her breath away. Out of nowhere, she felt tightness in her chest, and she struggled to breathe when she realized in a flash that she could lose him forever. Her knees weakened, her eyes burning as the uncontrollable floodgate of misery broke free, wave after wave of uncontrollable, soundless agony. Brad hugged her close. "Shh, it's okay, Diana. It's going to be okay." He just held her and let her weep.

CHAPTER Seven

Diana felt a hand nudge her arm. She instantly stiffened and sat up, blinking, and placed her hand over her heart, pressing the other into a kinked muscle at the side of her neck. How long had she been asleep? It seemed the whole family was there. Rodney was standing in front of her, and Andy and Neil stood off by the window. It was Brad leaning over her, resting his hand on her arm. She blinked a couple times and heard "Ma ma ma." Danny was in Becky's arms. Diana staggered to her feet and reached for him.

Someone cleared their throat, and Diana hugged Danny and rested him on her hip.

She blinked again and realized the doctor was there. He stepped closer, his shirtfront damp. He yanked off the blue surgical cap. His gray hair, so neat before, was a damp mess. "Surgery went well. There was minimal bleeding on the brain. Considering how far he fell, he's lucky. The spinal cord was bruised. We won't know until Jed wakes up if there will be any paralysis."

"When will Jed wake up?" It was Rodney who stepped

forward and spoke in a deep voice. Becky, Jed's short, plump mother, slid her arm around Diana's waist and placed her other hand on Danny's head as he clutched Diana's old t-shirt.

"Brain injuries are tricky. We hope soon. Let's just see how the next twenty-four hours play out."

"Can I see my husband?" Diana asked.

"Can we see him?" Rodney glanced at Diana as he asked. He was a tall man, almost a head taller than the doctor. With all the large Friessen men crowding the waiting room, the doctor was having to look up at each of them.

"He's being moved to ICU now, and then you can see him, one at a time. Don't stay long."

"Diana, let me take Danny." Becky reached for Danny again.

Brad and Rodney followed the doctor down the hall. They paused and glanced Diana's way, waiting for her. Becky stayed in the waiting room with Andy and Neil.

Rodney pressed his hand to Diana's shoulder and squeezed. "You need to eat something, Diana. You need rest, too, not just a nap on hard plastic chairs," he said.

Diana shook her head. "I want to see Jed. I need to make sure he's okay." She gazed up at her father-in-law, who had the same mysterious brown eyes as Jed, but older, with heavy lines on his face. He was a handsome man, and she struggled with her relationship with him. She'd never had a father. She didn't know how fathers and daughters talked, shared, or anything.

"We'll wait out here while you go in." Rodney dropped his hand, and Diana walked into the ICU, which was all floor-to-ceiling glass. Jed was still on a respirator, tubes and wires sticking out of him. A white bandage was wrapped around his head, and his eyes were still closed. She touched his hand, hoping he'd feel her and that it would be enough to wake him.

The dark-haired nurse on the other side watched her from where she adjusted some tubing. "Are you his wife?"

"Yes. How's he doing?" Diana asked.

"He's stable. You can hold his hand. Talk to him. If he moves or wakes up, let me know. I'll be right outside." She stepped out to the nurse's station.

Diana stood beside the bed. She slid her hand under Jed's, squeezing it and willing him again to wake up and squeeze hers back. But he still didn't move.

"I love you so much," she said. "I need you to come back to me. Danny needs you. He's here now, and your mom has him in the waiting room." She realized then that Jed wouldn't like that at all. The hospital waiting area was no place for a baby. "Your whole family is here." Diana nearly jumped when a hand pressed her shoulder. She turned to Rodney behind her.

"Danny's getting restless. Brad's reserved a room at a hotel nearby. Go get some sleep, have something to eat. I'll stay here with Jed."

Diana gazed at her baby boy in his grandma's arms as she now stood outside the glass door. Danny was fussing and reaching toward her. He needed her. Diana needed to eat. She knew that, too, but as she gazed back at her husband, she knew she couldn't leave, not yet.

"No, I can't leave. I'll nurse Danny in the waiting room. That should help for now, and then take Danny back to the hotel. Please."

Rodney must have seen her determination. "I'll stay with Jed while you go."

Diana stepped out of the room. "Becky, I'm just going to nurse Danny."

"Ma ma ma," Danny screeched as Becky handed him to his mother. He yanked at Diana's tangled hair.

"Owie, Danny, don't pull Mama's hair." She hugged him close.

"I'm going to go in and see Jed." Becky wandered in, went to the side of the bed, and bent over Jed. In that second, Diana saw how deeply Becky loved Jed. She loved Danny so much, so she understood a mother's love. It was just hard for her to see, as she'd always wanted a mother's love.

"Okay, Danny." Diana strode back to the waiting room, bouncing Danny on her hip as he noisily babbled.

Brad, Neil, and Andy all faced her from where they stood huddled in a circle. It was Brad who asked, "Everything okay? How's Jed?"

"He's apparently stable, but he didn't respond to me when I touched his hand or open his eyes when I talked to him."

Danny picked that moment to let out a howl, and he tried to flip sideways to nurse, his tiny hands clutching at her breasts.

Diana whipped her head around, looking for somewhere to sit that would be somewhat private to nurse him. "I *know*, Danny, okay?" Diana took the end seat closer to the window. She didn't look up as she slid her hand under her shirt and lifted her bra, trying to be inconspicuous as she cradled Danny's head so he could latch on and nurse, but Danny had other ideas, pushing her shirt up and exposing her pale breast, patting the fullness as he drank. Diana's cheeks burned and she dared not look up, but she wished for a blanket, even a jacket, to provide her some modesty. She slid around, even slouched a bit in desperation.

It was Neil, Jed's very neat and tidy, extremely handsome brother, with short styled hair, tan slacks, and a black silk sports shirt, who said, “Diana, here’s my jacket. It looks like my nephew is a chip off the old block and takes after every one of the Friessen males as an exhibitionist, with no thought as to his mama’s feelings.” Neil draped the jacket over her shoulder, and Diana gripped the front to cover Danny’s head and her breasts. Neil sat beside her, flashing a bright smile, his brown eyes twinkling.

“My little brother, Jed, do you all remember when he was fifteen and he helped himself to Mom and Dad’s wine collection? Took a bottle of some really expensive private reserve chardonnay got wasted with a couple of friends.”

“I never heard about that.” Andy laughed from where he leaned against the window.

“Yeah, just ask Brad what happened when Dad and Mom invited over the president of the cattleman’s association, with his young wife with the big boobs.”

Brad chuckled. “She was an eyeful. I remember her in that skimpy top that left little to the imagination. Mom asked once if she was chilly and wanted a sweater. Dad ogled her all of two seconds, and mom flicked his ear.” All three men laughed over that picture.

Diana felt herself let go of her earlier discomfort.

“So what about the wine?” Diana smiled, and then Danny smacked his lips and tried to twist to the other breast. Neil must have noticed, as he held his jacket up as she turned Danny, offering him her other breast. “Thank you,” she said as she glanced at Neil. He genuinely made her feel relaxed and eased her anxiety.

“My pleasure, Diana.” He winked at her and then continued on. “Now, by the time dinner came around and we were seated at the dining room table, Dad was opening a bottle of wine and poured everyone a glass. I remember watching the cattleman’s wife—I don’t even remember her name, but she took a sip and made this awful face. She set down her glass just as Dad sat at the head of the table and Mom carried in the platter of steak, and she said, 'This is water.'

"Of course, Mom rolled her eyes in a way I've never seen her do before and said, 'It is not. This is one of my favorites. It has a sharp, fruity taste.' It was from a trip that she'd taken with Dad to the Napa Valley on a wine tour. So Mom picked up her glass to prove this young lady wrong about the same time Dad did, and they both took a swallow. Mom's eyes widened…."

Diana glanced over at Brad, who was laughing so hard he had to sit. Andy's chest shook from laughing, and he was holding his stomach.

Neil winked at Diana as he continued in that deep, animated voice of his: "And then I looked over at Jed, and his face was white, his eyes big as saucers. And then I hear Mom say, in an extremely calm voice, 'Rodney, this is water.' And she set her glass down, and Dad and the president of the cattlemen's association both stared at the bottle, each taking a turn reading the label. And that loudmouth rancher was telling Dad to call the winery because someone sure needed to get fired, and all the while Jed is staring at the wine bottle. I know he's done something, and it was Mom and her sharp gaze that studied each of us as if she could read our minds, and she landed on Jed. I was positive she'd say something. She opened her mouth, exhaled hard, and then seemed to gather herself and said in this really calm voice, 'Brad, run down and grab another bottle of wine, red this time, since we are having beef. We may as well get something right.' "

Diana was now laughing. "Well, what happened? Your mom didn't say anything to Jed?"

Neil shook his head. "One thing about Mom, she'd

never embarrass one of us in front of a bunch of strangers. She saved that for the moment they walked out the door, which was about the time Jed knew he was busted. So he's doing the dishes, cleaning the kitchen. Mom stops and sees him scurrying around. Brad and I stayed where we were at the dining room table, waiting for the show. But Mom walks in, sees Jed, and says nothing. Instead, she kissed each of us on the cheek and said, 'Goodnight. I'm going to have a hot bath, and then I think I'll read for a bit.' And she said to Dad, who lingered in the living room, 'Rodney, make sure you take the wine to the liquor store tomorrow and file a complaint, and make sure they analyze the contents. Then we'll be sure to contact the winery, as someone will lose their job over this.' By this time, Jed's damn near freaking out. Remember, Brad, when he came into the dining room and stared at that wine bottle that was still filled with water sitting on the buffet?"

Brad was still laughing.

Neil, with flair, extended his hand over to Brad as he stared at Diana. "And Jed was absolutely trembling when he slunk over to big brother and said, 'Brad, I did something really stupid,' and he was shaking as he confessed to you that he stole the wine and he and his friend drank it, and just in case Mom and Dad counted the bottles of wine, he filled it with water, jammed the cork back in, and slipped it back into the wine rack. And do you remember what you said to him?"

Brad wiped his damp eye. "Yeah, I said to him, 'You're in big trouble. If I were you, I'd come clean.' "

"But he didn't. You remember how he practically waited on Mom, helped her with dinner, jumping up every night and telling her to sit, he'd do the dishes. And we knew Mom knew, but she never said a word. She'd smile at

Jed, thank him for his thoughtfulness. Do you remember how long it went on for?"

"Four wonderful days." Becky strode in, and it was then that Diana noticed Becky's wrinkled slacks and the creases in her blouse, a sadness lurking in her warm eyes. "He did everything for me, appearing at my side, bringing me tea and asking if there was anything else he could do for me. When he started scrubbing the kitchen floor, I had to let him off. In good conscience, no matter what he did, the guilt was eating away at him. I hoped he would've confessed, but … Jed was determined to punish himself. I was starting to feel so guilty with how hard he was working with school, homework, chores, and then being my personal slave. I called him in, told him to put away the mop, and sat him down. And I finally told him I knew that it was him who filled the wine bottle with water."

Danny pushed away then and sat up. Diana adjusted her bra and shirt clumsily. Danny was now rubbing his eyes.

"Oh, my sweet boy, come on over to Grandma." He went to her willingly. "Jed always held on to everything, even when he did something wrong. You all did, but Jed even more so. He's always been a lone wolf."

Silence filled the waiting room as everyone seemed lost in thought. The lighthearted teasing Neil had so easily weaved disappeared.

"Thank you, Neil." Diana stood the weariness and worry making her legs feel like two stiff tree stumps. "Becky, would you mind taking Danny back to the hotel? I want to stay with Jed. I can't go until I know he's going to be okay."

"I can stay with Diana. Rodney, Neil, Brad, if you want to go to the hotel, I can call you." Andy stepped closer to Diana.

Diana had opened her mouth to say something when Brad stiffened. Even the expression on his face was similar to how Jed had looked the time the local hay guy showed up with a truck full of moldy hay, trying to pass it off as top grade.

A lock of hair drooped in her eyes, and she quickly swept it back behind her ears.

"No, Andy, I'll stay. You've done so much already, driving back to get Danny, too. I'm the single one here with nowhere to go. You should get back to Laura, your wife. She has to be worried, wondering what's going on," Neil said as he accepted his coat back from Diana.

"Andy, you come back to the hotel with us. Get some rest first. Neil will stay with Diana." It was Rodney who stepped in and patted Andy's back.

"Dad, I'll stay, too. You three take Danny to the hotel." Brad stood with his brother Neil. The two of them together appeared, in their own way, a formidable force.

Before Diana could say anything, Brad was ushering her to Jed's room. She paused at the glass door and looked up at her brother-in-law, and what she saw rattled her. It was what she believed was a big-brother protectiveness for her.

A HAND PRESSED against Diana's head, and she bolted upright. She'd dozed off in a chair she'd pulled up to Jed's bed, resting her head on the bed as she held his hand. She blinked as she sat up and then stood when she realized it was Jed's hand touching her—Jed's golden brown eyes watching her.

"Hi, you're awake." She leaned over and kissed his forehead. Diana glanced at Rodney, who was sleeping in the chair on the other side of the bed. She'd been unaware he'd returned. "Rodney," she called out.

He opened his eyes and must have noticed something in her expression, as he jerked forward and stood up, taking Jed's other hand. "You scared the life out of us, son. I'll get the doctor." Rodney hurried out of the room.

Jed was still hooked up to the respirator. He tried to move and touched the tube taped to his mouth. Just then, the doctor brushed past her. She stepped back and watched as he shone a light in Jed's eyes. Two nurses followed. "Jed, I want you to squeeze my hand if you understand me."

Jed squeezed his hand and then gestured to the tube down his throat.

"We're going to take the tube out. Just give us a minute."

Rodney put his arm around Diana as they moved back and watched as he was taken off the respirator. Jed gagged when the tube was pulled out. Then his vitals were checked by the nurse.

The doctor moved to the foot of the bed, lifted the sheet. "Jed, I want you to tell me if you feel this?" He pulled a pen from his shirt pocket and poked Jed's instep, sliding it sharply and quickly upward.

"Yeah." Jed's voice was rough and gravelly as he wiggled his large foot.

Jed sought Diana out with his gaze. Her eyes burned, and her chest ached from the fears she'd been holding on to. She nodded, and her lips trembled just as he held out his hand to her. She went to him as the doctor said, "Jed, this is good news. You gave us all quite a scare. I'll be back to check on you." The doctor turned to Rodney and said, "He's doing good. If his vitals stay strong, we should be able to move him from the ICU tomorrow."

"Thank you, Doctor," Diana felt the need to say.

He nodded and smiled. "You need to get some rest. Your husband still has some recovery time ahead of him, but you have a baby and a husband, and you'll be no good to anyone if you let yourself get run down."

"I'll make sure she gets something to eat and some rest." Rodney placed both hands on Diana's shoulders and squeezed gently in support.

"See that she does." The doctor left, and Diana leaned down and kissed Jed.

"I love you so much.... Oh, Jed."

She rested her head on his chest as tears nearly blinded her. He pressed his hand to her wild mane of red hair and ran his fingers through the unruly waves, which had long since come free from her ponytail, and she hadn't once tried to fix them.

"It's okay, baby. Don't cry. Where's Danny?" His voice was gravelly, and just then, a nurse walked in with a cup and straw.

"I'll get you to take a sip of water, Jed."

Diana reached for the cup from the nurse before she could slip the straw to his lips. "I'll give it to him." The nurse hesitated for a minute but then smiled and handed the cup to Diana.

Jed frowned as she held it to him.

"Drink, Jed."

He swallowed, licked his lips, and said, "What was that about?"

Diana felt her cheeks pinken. She knew she had acted territorial, and she knew Jed had seen it. "I'm just tired, and—"

"And what, Diana?"

"I didn't want her helping you. I know it sounds silly, and it does to me now, as I say it. But you're my husband."

He smiled at her. "Yes, I am. Now answer me: Where's Danny?"

"Your mom took him back to the hotel. He was tired, just like your wife here." Rodney stood beside Diana and again rested his hand on her shoulder. "Except your wife refuses to leave you and hasn't eaten a thing. Maybe you can talk some sense into her."

Jed narrowed his eyes. "Dad, take Diana back to the hotel. Make sure she gets something to eat, and don't let her come back until she does. Diana, Danny needs you, and you have to look after yourself. If I could get out of this bed right now, I'd take you back there myself."

Diana said nothing for the longest time until Jed squeezed her hand again. "Diana, I know you so well. You're exhausted. I promise you I'm not going anywhere."

"I don't want to leave you alone. You scared me," she whispered.

It was Rodney who said, "Brad's in the waiting room. He's been waiting to come in here and spend time with Jed."

"Brad's here?" Jed said in a tone that sounded a little like surprise.

"Jed, your whole family's here. Your mom and dad, Neil, too, even Andy," Diana muttered as Jed gazed first at her, then at his father.

"Andy left, Diana," Rodney said. "He had to get back to his wife. But Neil's back at the hotel now. Brad's been here the entire time. He's out in the waiting room."

Something passed between father and son. "Diana, Dad will take you back to the hotel. Go with him. Dad, can you send Brad in? I want to talk to him."

Rodney rested his palm on Diana's shoulder. "Come on, Diana."

She quickly leaned down and kissed Jed again. "I love you. I'll be back soon."

"I love you, and don't come back until you've eaten and gotten some rest." He watched her with a heavy-lidded gaze that let her know very well that he meant every word he said.

"I'm not going to argue, Jed. I'll go back, get some rest, and be with Danny, but I'm coming right back." She squeezed his hand and then allowed Rodney to lead her out. What she didn't miss was the look that passed again between father and son, which her tired brain could make no sense of.

Rodney paused in the doorway and said, "I'll send Brad in."

CHAPTER *Eight*

To say the hotel was attractive was like saying a Porsche was a nice, modest car for commuting. It was both lavish and way out of Diana's budget. The hotel room was situated on the top floor—the only floor you needed a key card to access.

A bellman waited outside the elevator in a red uniform jacket and black pants. "Mister Friessen, welcome back, sir."

"Thank you. Ben, is it?" Rodney asked with genuine interest.

"Yes, sir. Ben it is, sir."

"This is my daughter-in-law, Diana. She'll be staying with us."

"Is there any luggage I can bring up?" the young man asked eagerly.

Diana dropped her gaze to the faded filthy jeans she'd never worn off their ranch and had been in since yesterday. Even her sneakers were old and frayed. She knew she looked a mess, could even pass for someone off the street, and she felt her cheeks burn. She had been aware of every eye on her from the moment she strode through the lavish lobby among the upscale guests.

It was a reminder of the wealth that belonged to Jed's family, which Jed had no part of, and it still made Diana uncomfortable. "No luggage for me, sorry. Just the clothes on my back." She realized she sounded quite sharp.

"Diana, let's get you some food ordered. Ben, thank you again." Rodney didn't appear fazed by her rudeness. He slid his key card into a large double door, one of three on the floor, and opened it into a grand living room, with floor-to-ceiling windows, a gas fireplace, a huge dining room, and what looked like three separate bedrooms. The carpeting was white plush, and everything in this suite appeared golden, crystal, and very expensive. Neil was sitting at a desk in an alcove just off this grand living room, talking on the phone. Diana froze and didn't know what to do, where to sit, where to go. Her whole body ached.

"Oh, Diana, there you are. Brad phoned and told me the good news that Jed's awake. He also said Rodney finally convinced you to leave." She opened her arms and hugged Diana, and Diana stiffened, but Becky wouldn't let her go. She pulled back only to wrap her arm around Diana's waist and lead her to one of the bedrooms. Diana relaxed and leaned into Becky. She knew Jed's mother really did care for her, and she made it so easy. Diana did love her, and she wanted the motherly concern that the other woman was showing, but she didn't know how to accept it, and the money thing made her really uncomfortable.

"I hope you don't mind, Diana, but I had some clothes sent up for you. I had to guess on your size. If it doesn't fit, I'll have it sent back and get you something that fits."

The bedroom Becky walked her into was larger than their house, with a king-size bed and an enormous en suite.

The windows were again floor to ceiling and filled one entire wall, with another fireplace in the bedroom.

"Oh my God, Becky. This is just so much. You didn't have to do that. I'll pay you back… but I don't think we can afford this… and this room..."

She gave Diana an odd look and frowned. "My dear girl, Rodney and I aren't just Jed's parents. You and that beautiful grandson are our family. You are our responsibility, and there isn't anything we wouldn't give you. We are looking after you now, so let us, Diana." Becky slid her arm around her waist as Diana choked on a sob. She then sat with her on the bed when Diana couldn't fight the exhausted tears of the last twenty-four hours.

"I'm so sorry. I didn't mean to lose it like that." Diana apologized as she wiped her eyes and realized Rodney was in the doorway.

"Diana, I took the liberty of ordering you some room service," Rodney said. "Is there anything else I can get for you?"

"No, but thank you, Rodney." Diana swiped at her nose.

Becky patted her back. "Diana, why don't you go have a bath before room service arrives? Rodney, those clothes I ordered for Diana, are they in the living room?"

"The bags are on the sofa. I'll go get them." Rodney strode away.

"Becky, you didn't have to buy me clothes, too."

"Go get in the bath now. We've already settled this."

Diana strode into the large bathroom and shut the door. Her eyes widened at the marble countertops, the huge Jacuzzi tub, and the glassed-in shower that had four showerheads and would probably fit the whole family. She'd never had such luxury. She strode up the three steps to the large tub and started filling it. Steam filled the bathroom. On the counter were soaps, bath salts, shampoo, even a hair brush. Diana wasted no time, kicking off her shoes and peeling off her clothes. She brushed her hair and then climbed in the steamy bath, allowing the heat to ease the stiffness that knotted her muscles.

A knock on the door had her sitting up.

"Diana, it's Becky. The clothes are on your bed. And room service just arrived with the food. Don't stay in there too long."

"Okay," she said.

She quickly washed her hair and scrubbed herself clean. She stepped out of the bath and dried herself, pulling on a thick white robe on the back of the door, and ran a brush through her wet hair, feeling much better and very tired.

She pulled open the door and smiled at the new clothes on the bed, a pair of nice blue lounging pants with matching jacket, underwear, socks, two-piece pajamas and casual slacks with a couple bright t-shirts. Diana opted for the pajamas, since she planned to crawl into bed right after she ate. She pulled the robe on overtop, pulled on a pair of socks, and opened the door.

"Ma ma ma." Danny clapped his chubby hands and grinned at Diana. Neil bounced him in his arms.

"You are going to let your mama eat, and then she's going to sleep and you get to hang with your uncle." Neil didn't let Diana hover. He wrapped his arm around her shoulder and led her to the dining room and to the table filled with food.

"Sit, sit. You'll eat, then go to bed," said Becky as they made her sit. She lifted a silver plate warmer with an omelet that smelled heavenly, and Diana ate.

CHAPTER *Nine*

It had been eight days since the accident, Diana spent every waking moment at the hospital with Jed. Rodney and Becky cared for Danny, and Neil chauffeured her to and from the hospital. Brad returned home two days after surgery, when Jed woke up. The first day after regaining consciousness, he had slid out of bed and walked to the bathroom.

Diana lounged in a vinyl chair in Jed's hospital room in the new sweat suit Becky had bought for her. The way Jed had watched her when she walked in that morning with Neil, and listened quietly as Neil joked and teased, she knew something wasn't right. "What's wrong, Jed?"

He lay in bed in the t-shirt and sweatpants she'd brought in yesterday. "That another new outfit? I noticed you have a lot of new clothes. Who bought them?"

"Ah, your mom did. I didn't pack anything when we came, Jed. I haven't been home to get any clothes. Danny and I have been here. You know that."

"Well, don't get used to it," Jed snapped.

Diana felt as if she'd just been slapped. "Jed, your mom

and dad are just trying to help, is all. You're not being fair to me, and you know I'm not like that."

"And this private room," he swept his hand around the small room, "I don't have coverage for this. Who's paying for it?"

The door opened, and in strode Rodney, dressed in slacks and a yellow golf shirt that showed off his tan nicely. His short stylish white hair had been freshly cut.

Jed frowned and turned away. Rodney glanced at Diana with a puzzled expression before saying, "How are you feeling this morning, son?"

"Fine," Jed snapped.

Diana raised her eyebrows and then moved out of her chair, slipping beside him until he was forced to look at her. She stared at him, letting her disapproval sink in until he shut his eyes.

"Sorry, I just want to get out of here, get home. Diana, I got things to do. What about the kids we had booked to start riding? They were supposed to start already."

"Jed, I called each of them and told them about the accident and that we had to postpone for now. All except one is willing to wait," said Diana.

"Jed, your mom and I will stay as long as you need us. We'll help get this center of yours opened. What needs to be done?" Rodney asked. Diana noted he wasn't taking control, as Jed wouldn't stand for that. Rodney obviously knew his son well.

"You and mom have done enough. I can't have you doing all this for me and Diana. For God's sake, even Andy is looking after our place and the horses. We're going to owe him for that, too."

Diana gripped Jed's arm and squeezed. "Jed, don't be rude—"

Rodney cut her off. "Diana, it's okay. Jed, we're family.

You don't owe family for helping out. It's time you realized that."

The door opened again, and the doctor strode in, wearing a white coat over a shirt and tie, with dark dress pants. "How are you doing this morning, Jed?" He flipped through the chart at the foot of the bed.

"Doc, when can I go home?"

The doctor glanced at Jed and said nothing for several seconds. "Well, there are some things we need to discuss...."

"No, Doc, when can I get out of here? I feel fine. I want to go home."

Diana glanced over at Rodney, who frowned back at her.

"Jed, why don't you let the doctor finish what he needs to say? You have some serious injuries, son, which are going to take time to heal." Rodney was finally sounding frustrated.

"Actually, Jed's healed nicely from his injuries. As long as he doesn't climb any ladders, do any heavy lifting or overdo it, he should be able to go home in a week." The doctor once again glanced at Jed as if he wanted to say more.

Diana took one look at Jed and knew he'd never last another week in the hospital. The doctor must have, too. "Okay, why don't we say a few more days?"

Jed turned to Diana. "I want you to take Danny home today. If I'm getting out in a few days, I want you home now. You're hanging around here, and there is nothing to do but stare at a ceiling and keep me company. Danny needs you."

Diana opened her mouth to argue, but Jed cut her off. "Diana, come on, honey. Take Danny home. Please."

"Can Jed really come home that soon?" Diana asked the doctor.

The doctor wrote something on the chart. "As long as he promises to take it easy, he can."

"All right, we'll go home, but I'll be back to pick you up."

"Wow, I never thought I could miss a place so much." Diana shut the rear passenger door of the luxury SUV Neil had rented. Rodney was in the front seat. Danny was asleep in the car seat in back between Diana and Becky.

A young cowboy wandered out of the barn, wearing a jean jacket and pushing a wheelbarrow filled with old straw and manure.

It should have been Diana hurrying over to thank Andy's ranch hand for helping out, but Rodney stepped over, shook the young man's hand, and spoke with him.

Diana gazed at the six horses in the distance, grazing in the fenced-off pasture on the other side of the barn.

"I think someone else is happy to be home." Becky lifted Danny from his car seat. "And hungry, too, I think." Danny shoved his fist in his mouth and was smacking his lips, squawking in the baby talk he'd started the past week. Diana, for a moment, wondered if her mothering skills were lacking, as he'd flourished under Becky's care.

Diana was aware that one of the reasons Jed wanted them home was so Rodney and Becky wouldn't spend any more money on her and Danny. She knew he felt beholden, and she'd never told him how lavish the hotel suite was, because she worried about how he'd react. She'd offered to pay, but Rodney would hear none of it and insisted on paying for everything. Maybe that was why Jed had pushed and insisted she go home with Danny.

"Diana," Neil called out to her and waved her over to where he stood with Rodney and the young cowboy.

"I'll take Danny inside, heat up some pears for him. Is the door locked?" asked Becky as she stepped up to the door and turned the knob.

It opened and Diana shrugged. "We never worry much around here."

Diana hurried over to Neil and Rodney just as the cowboy climbed in a beat-up old pickup and drove away.

"That was Andy's ranch hand. Andy has been here, too, and they finished the roof of the barn," said Rodney.

Diana glanced at the newly shingled roof, and a picture of Jed flashed in her mind as he turned to her and then stepped on the ladder and fell. She shut her eyes and swallowed. "Jed's not going to like that. He doesn't want to owe people."

"We're not people, Diana, we're *family*. And don't you worry about Jed. After I talk with him, he'll relax."

Diana looked at Neil and the mischievous glint in his deep brown eyes and frowned.

"Well, at least he'll lighten up a bit." Neil slung his arm around Diana's shoulder and hugged her much like a brother does. "Right, Dad?"

Rodney just shook his head and gazed at the barn and over at the riding ring that was still missing posts. "What else needs to be done, Diana? Walk me through it. Jed won't be doing much around here for a while yet."

"We need to finish the riding ring. Those posts over there still need to be put in and fenced off. He was supposed to get a cover up at least so we could still work with the kids when it rains, but for now that can wait." Diana strode into the barn beside Neil and Rodney, and of course Rodney saw the two stalls with a missing latch. There was rope instead to hold it closed.

"Some repair work in here needs done." Neil strode into the boxlike tack room stuffed with the saddles, halters, blankets, and everything they used and needed for the horses. In the corner, she noticed the box of riding helmets for the kids. Even though the kids were supposed to have their own, they needed to expect some would show up without one.

"Some of this stuff has seen better days." Neil rummaged through the tack box. "There is a lot to do here to get this place open. I think we need to hire some help. Dad, you and I can help finish the barn. What do you think?" Rodney glanced down at Diana. She knew he was aware of her unease, because Jed would have none of it. When she'd suggested hiring earlier, before the accident, he'd flat-out said no and had nearly bitten her head off.

"Diana, someone's on the phone for you," Becky shouted from the house.

"Excuse me," she said and hurried inside.

Becky handed her the phone. Danny was strapped in his highchair, pureed pears smeared in his hair and on his face, and he smiled brightly as if pleased by what he'd done.

"Hello, this is Diana."

"Mrs. Friessen, this is First National Bank. We've left several messages for your husband, Jed Friessen," the woman barked in a sharp, irritated voice.

"My husband had an accident and fell off a ladder. He's in the hospital in Seattle, and I just got home. Is there something I can help you with?" Diana watched Danny as he clapped and squealed to his grandma, who wiped his face and then lifted him from the high chair and carried him down the hall.

"Your husband is over sixty days in arrears on the mortgage. Until now, he's maintained the late payments, barely, through the last six months. The line of credit he took out two months ago is maxed out, and he hasn't made a payment on it yet."

In that moment, everything seemed to come to a full stop after what the woman said finally sank in. "What? I don't understand. I knew money was tight, but that's impossible.... What line of credit? I didn't know Jed took out a line of credit." She must have been speaking loudly, because Becky was suddenly beside her, frowning.

"Can I get back to you?" Diana asked, because she needed to figure out what was going on. She needed some answers before she said one more thing to this banker.

She scribbled down the banker's name and phone number and promised to call back before the end of the day, which was two hours from now and didn't give her a lot of time.

When she looked up at Becky, she said, "Jed's been hiding some things from me. Apparently we're broke. That was the bank. I have to call them back. I need to talk to Jed." She turned in a circle, placed her hands on her hips, and then looked over at Becky again.

"Diana..." Becky started to say something and then shared a meaningful look. Becky was a smart woman and knew her son well. He was a man you had to be careful with.

Diana knew Jed would be furious that his mom knew anything about his business. He didn't share his problems with anyone, apparently not even Diana, his wife. But these were her problems, too, and she somehow needed to get that through Jed's thick skull.

"Becky, can you watch Danny? Jed keeps all his papers in the office in the back of the barn. I need to go have a look and figure out where to begin to fix this." Diana strode to the door and yanked it open.

"Diana… I know you know Jed, but be careful how you handle this. Pride, with a man like Jed, is a powerful thing."

Diana glanced at Becky, and what she saw was wariness and worry etched in the deep lines around her light eyes. Diana nodded and hopped down the wooden steps, still missing a handrail, and hurried to the barn as her own confused feelings of love, mixed with frustration and the big old unknown that had clouded her good sense, began to dissipate.

CHAPTER *Ten*

Diana didn't know how long she sat behind the old bargain-store desk, with bank statements, papers, and overdue notices sprawled over the desktop. She'd rummaged through the drawers and pulled everything out, but now the room was a mass of shadows, and she had to squint to read the numbers.

A boot scraped, and someone cleared their throat behind her. Diana startled and scooted around to see her brother-in-law Brad hovering in the doorway. He leaned against the door jamb and then scratched his head, wincing as he watched her. Diana took a deep breath, smelling the fresh hay and horse manure, and listened to the horses, now back in the barn stalls, munching on hay.

Diana rubbed her eyes, which burned from reading fine print and numbers, notices, and zero balances. She had a pretty good idea now of the financial mess they were in, and she wondered how Jed had managed to hide all of this. She leaned back in the stiff wooden chair.

"What are you doing back here, Brad?" Diana felt

numb, tired, and pretty beat up as she gazed up, wondering why Brad was here.

"Neil picked me up. I just flew in. Listen, Diana, I love my brother. He's about as pigheaded as all of us. But he's family, and you're family. And family sticks together. At one time, Jed and I were about as far apart as two brothers could get. Never talked for years, and I blamed him for something he didn't do."

Brad pushed away from the wall, shoved his hands in his faded jean pockets, and stepped around the cluttered desk to sit on the edge. "My first marriage was a disaster. Well… let's just say I've grown up a lot, but I was more interested in how a woman looked hanging off my arm, with all that flash and glitter, and I wanted Crystal—except she was about as faithful and trustworthy as a tomcat is to a rat. She was a drama queen who was never happy unless everyone else around her was miserable. She didn't like the closeness of my family, and she figured she could have both me and Jed. Let's just say she played us against each other, and I said some things to Jed I'll never forgive myself for. Even after she left… with all the trouble she caused, I never reached out to Jed, even though I knew deep down she'd played us both. It was Emily, my wife now, who helped bring my family together."

Brad looked away, and Diana wanted to reach out and touch his arm, ease the guilt she could see he still carried for his brother. "I didn't know any of that. Jed never told me."

Brad was in shadows as he stared down at Diana. "Jed was hurt real bad, and it was partly my fault. Jed always did things his own way, but after that he walked away from the family, made his own way. I admire him and his pigheaded determination, but I'm also careful with him now. I respect him. I've also seen how much he loves you, and he'll die to protect you and Danny. Jed doesn't take kindly to anyone getting into his business."

Diana reached for one of the folded papers on the desk. She handed it to Brad. "This is how much Jed's in arrears on the mortgage." She reached for another letter on the pile in front of her. "This is from the state about the grant I thought we had for start-up costs for the therapeutic riding. Apparently, funding was pulled, so where Jed was getting the money from put us here…" Diana reached for another pile of papers on the desk. "These are the bank statements, line of credit, all the credit cards. Everything's maxed out." She allowed the papers to fall from her hand and onto the desk. "We're broke. There's no money coming in. So, evidently, my husband was so stressed out he wasn't sleeping. When I asked him what was wrong, he wouldn't tell me. He was killing himself: the barn roof, the riding ring, the horses for me. We didn't have the money to do it. So when he stepped onto that ladder, stressed and tired, it was because of me that I damn near lost… him." Her voice trembled as a sob caught high in her throat, and she pressed shaky fingertips to her lips. Her eyes burned, but she wouldn't let a tear fall as she forced a smile to her lips.

Brad stared with deep concern for her. "This isn't your fault, Diana." Brad still held the letter from the bank. He briefly read it, lips firm, and looked back at her. "I'll talk some sense into Jed. It's why I came back." Brad was a handsome man, solidly built, just like Jed, but older, in a different way.

"I can't let you do that, Brad. Jed's my husband. I respect him. I'm really mad at him right now, and he'll be angry that I know about this.… He'll be furious that you know." She took a deep breath and stood up. "I need to go talk to my husband. I was supposed to call the banker back at four, and I didn't because I didn't know what to say."

Brad didn't say anything for several seconds. In the dimness, she couldn't make out what he was thinking, not that she could read his mind, but she was pretty good at reading people's expressions and knowing how they were feeling. Brad was so much like Jed in that way, both men who hid everything, as if they thought that would somehow insulate their women.

"It'll be late by the time we get there, but I'll drive you."

Diana saw then, in the way he stepped toward her, that he too had a few things to say to Jed.

"Let me check on Danny," she shivered in the cool night air and rubbed her bare arms, "and grab my coat."

CHAPTER Eleven

"Jed, I'm not going to keep arguing with you. You should have told me." Diana sat on the edge of Jed's hospital bed. The metal rail lowered as his hand rested across her thigh and his dark eyes flared with a fire she hadn't seen before.

"Diana, stop. I'll take care of the bank when I get out of here. You're not going to work. You've got Danny to look after. Don't you think he deserves a mother at home? Haven't I looked after everything? It's my responsibility to look after you and Danny."

She knew he wasn't hearing her. He pressed the power button to raise the bed at the head until he was almost sitting up. Diana glanced at the closed door, where Brad waited on the other side.

"Jed, I'm your wife. You're supposed to share everything with me, and you're hiding things. I knew you weren't sleeping and something was bothering you. I had no idea the state pulled the grant. I never would have pushed for the therapeutic riding. I thought we had the grant, the money. You stepped onto that ladder, exhausted, busting your butt for me, and could have been killed, and then where would Danny and I be?"

"Diana, nothing's going to happen to me. Doc says I can get out of here by the end of the week. I already told you I'll handle it." He rubbed her leg with his large, chafed hand.

She rested her hand over his and pressed it to her stomach. "I'm pregnant again, Jed. I knew I was late. I picked up a pregnancy test in the hospital gift shop a few days ago, and it was positive. Jed, I can work from home, handle small estate stuff, and still look after Danny. We're supposed to be a team, Jed, working together. So let me help, because I don't ever want to be standing, watching you fall and lying hurt, not knowing if you're dead or alive."

Jed wiped the tear sliding down her cheek. "You're pregnant, really?" He smiled when he asked it, but he wasn't fooling her. She could see the shadow of worry dimming the brightness in his eyes.

A knock on the door had her looking up, and Brad stepped in. "Am I interrupting?"

Jed looked over, but Diana was irritated because she could sense Jed's relief.

"Diana, can you run down to the cafeteria and grab me a slice of pie?"

"What? Why on earth would you want pie from the hospital? If you wanted pie, I could have made you one at home." She didn't move from her spot, but he nudged her hand, giving her one of his crooked smiles.

"Please, honey."

"Fine, I'll get you your pie." She started toward the door, glanced at Brad, and didn't miss the look he gave Jed.

"Apple, Diana, please," Jed called out before she stepped out the door.

"Pie in a hospital? That's pretty lame." Brad yanked the vinyl-covered chair from the corner and slid it closer to the bed, lowering his large frame down and stretching out his long legs. "So, out with it. What don't you want Diana to hear?"

"You drove her all the way to Seattle tonight. What did she tell you?" Jed stared at his big brother, a brother he'd always looked up to, even after the lies Crystal told. She had been a sexy, deceitful woman who fooled Jed at first, but the rift she set between him and Brad seemed to be a scar that hadn't quite healed, even now.

Brad clasped his hands together and rested them on his large brass buckle. "If you're fishing around, trying to find out whether Diana told us about your financial trouble, we know. And don't go blaming her. Mom answered the phone. Diana was mighty thrown when the bank called. Mom called me—she's worried about how you'll react. Dad knows, too, and Neil."

Jed shut his eyes as a wave of shame washed over him. He hated when anyone got in his business, any part of it, and for his parents and brothers to think he couldn't look after his wife and kid, with another on the way, he couldn't stand it.

"Knock it off, Jed. No one's thinking less of you. How could we? You're the only one of us who struck out on your own. You never took anything from Dad, even what he set aside for you, as he'd done for each of us. I got the ranch handed to me, and Neil's with dad and that big ranching venture they've started down on the Yucatan peninsula. And you… don't think I'm not a little envious of your guts to build something from the dirt, from nothing," Brad growled.

Jed turned his head a little too fast and was hit by a wave of dizziness.

"You okay?" The chair scraped back, and Brad leaned over Jed. "I'll go grab the doctor."

"No, I'm fine. Just moved a little too fast." Brad seemed to hesitate and glanced at the door. "Really, Brad, I'm fine. Listen, I want to talk to you before Diana gets back. I don't want her worrying about anyone taking anything from us, like our home. She had a rough time as a kid, and that kind of hurt, of having everything ripped away, sticks. I still see it sometimes, a thoughtless comment from someone who should know better. She hides it, all those painful shadows that still haunt her."

Brad said nothing, just stared at Jed, rubbing his thumb over his lip, then slowly nodded. "I saw the letters. Diana went through your papers, the letter from the bank, the state taking the grant. You're in arrears big time. We only want to help. If I tried to give you money, you wouldn't take it, would you?"

Jed had a lot to consider. "I'll think about it."

That must have surprised Brad, as his eyes widened and he started to say something when the door pushed open, and in walked Diana, carrying a plate with a piece of pie wrapped in plastic.

She set the pie on the bedside table with the fork. "There was no apple, so I got you cherry."

Jed reached for her hand and pulled her toward him until she sat on the bed beside him. "Diana's pregnant." He rested his hand on her stomach.

"Jed, it's too soon to tell anyone," Diana admonished.

Brad grinned. "That's great news."

Jed swallowed and stared at his wife, who watched him in a way that bared her heart to him. She trusted him. She loved him with a fiery passion that left no doubt she'd walk through fire for him. However, the financial mess they were in was the least of his worries. What she still didn't know, and what he couldn't tell her, would break her heart, and Jed also knew she would never forgive him.

CHAPTER
Twelve

Jed stared at the wheelchair parked beside his hospital bed. He was sitting on the edge of the bed, dressed in blue jeans and a brown flannel shirt, waiting for Diana to pick him up, because today he was going home. Today he'd finally see his baby boy, hold him, rock him, and play with him.

The door pushed open and Doctor Gordon strode in. She was a tall, dark-haired woman in her early thirties, with the most amazing shade of brown eyes that filled with passion every time she spoke. She wore a long white doctor's coat over a pair of black slacks and black shirt. She watched Jed for a minute before kicking the door stopper down with her foot, leaving it open just a crack. "So, today's the day. How does it feel to be going home?" She stopped in front of Jed and crossed her arms.

"Good. Can't wait to get out of here, see my boy. Hold my wife."

She nodded and tightened her lips. "You have to take it easy. No heavy lifting. Stay off your horse, lots of rest, just like Doctor Hardy told you—"

Jed cut her off. "I know the drill, Doc. Both you and Doctor Hardy said it over and over. But I'm not lying around doing nothing. I have a ranch to run. I'll do what I can."

"Jed, you're just walking, and I feel I need to warn you that if you push yourself too hard, you could be right back in here. You need to listen, Jed, to me and Doctor Hardy. You have a family to think of, and you know, Jed… that's not the only reason."

Jed didn't want to think about his conversation with Doctor Hardy. "I already told you—"

She cut *him* off this time, resting her hand on his shoulder, and sat beside him on the bed. "Jed, this isn't a death sentence. It doesn't have to be."

"Letting someone cut into a part of my brain, and with one slip of the knife I'm no longer a man, can't look after my family, and suddenly become a burden to be looked after like a baby every day by my wife? Are you kidding me? It's worse, and I'd never do that to Diana. She'd hate me, and she'd have every right to."

Doctor Gordon titled her head and slid her hand over his shoulder, touching his cheek with her other hand. "You haven't told her. My God, I can only imagine how she'd feel if she knew there was a chance. If you were my husband…"

The door banged, and Jed looked up. The doctor dropped her hand and stood up, jamming her hands in her coat pocket.

Diana stood in the doorway, arms crossed in front of her. Brad stood behind her. It wasn't so much Brad's questioning look that bothered him. It was the frown on Diana's face, the pained look in her eyes.

She wore a jean jacket over a pastel t-shirt, worn jeans, and her red hair was tied back in a ponytail. She stepped in the room and went right beside Jed. He wrapped his arm around her waist, and she said nothing.

"Well, if you need anything, let me know. The nurse will be in with your discharge papers, and then you're on your way." The doctor started to leave.

"Thank you, Doctor," said Diana in a curt tone, one she used the few times she did her lawyer thing, and she squeezed Jed's hand a little harder than usual.

The attractive doctor slipped past Brad. He took a second look at the slim young physician as he strode in and raised his eyebrows, and then he cleared his throat as he glanced back at Diana. "So, you ready to go home, little brother?"

"Can't wait to get out of here. To hold my boy, my wife." He pressed his hand possessively against Diana's waist, but she remained stiff and aloof, and he could feel the fire that stoked her temper simmering just below the surface.

Jed slid off the bed and stood up. "Let's go."

A nurse hurried in with a chart and then set the brakes on the wheelchair.

"You don't expect me to sit in that thing. I'm walking out of here."

The dark-haired, mousy-looking nurse glanced at Diana and swallowed as she stared back up at Jed, who towered over her.

"Jed, sit in the chair." Diana reached for the chart. "These the release papers?"

"Yes. If you can sign, please, and if your husband will sit in the chair, I'll wheel him out of here." The nurse spoke to Diana. She was obviously a smart lady who'd let Diana deal with the brute who was trying to intimidate her.

Brad yanked open the small closet. "You got everything packed?"

"It's all there in that duffel bag on the chair." Jed pointed to the green canvas bag.

Diana handed the chart back to the nurse and gestured to the chair, her shimmering blue eyes dancing with fire and passion. Then she snapped her fingers and said, "Sit down in the chair, Jed, because you're not walking out of here. There are policies in place, so decide whether you want to go home or stay and argue."

Brad chuckled behind him. Jed scowled and then sat in the small black chair. "Let's go. I want to get out of this place."

Diana led the way to the elevator, head high, walking with purpose. He could tell she was irritated. Brad carried the duffle bag, and the mousy nurse pushed the wheelchair.

It was three hours before Brad pulled down the dusty driveway leading to his ranch. Jed had chatted briefly with Brad before leaning the front seat back to sleep.

The squared-out dirt parking lot in front of the house seemed filled with vehicles: a couple of older pickups, an older flatbed, Andy's dark truck, a fancy SUV he presumed belonged to Neil, and his mom and dad's car.

"What the heck…?" Jed was speechless when he noticed that the once bare area he'd cleared for the new round ring for the lessons was filled with what looked like six guys carrying wood, ladders, working to construct a roof.

"Diana, what the hell is going on? Who are all these

guys, and what are they doing?" Jed turned in the leather seat to see his wife's wide eyes.

"Jed, don't be mad at Diana." Brad pulled in front of the small house and parked.

The front door flew open, and out stepped Becky, carrying Danny. Rodney followed behind. Jed glanced at Brad, then back at Diana. He yanked open the door and stepped out. He glanced at the workers and his brother Neil, who waved from the barn.

"Hey, little brother. Welcome home," Neil shouted and strode toward him.

Danny reached for Jed. His big eyes, for a moment, appeared frantic. Jed quickly reached for him and hugged him, deeply breathing his baby scent. "Oh, I missed you, Danny. Look how big you've grown." He kissed him again.

Danny reached up his chubby hand and patted Jed's chin, his cheek. "Da da."

"Did you hear that, Diana? He called me Daddy."

Diana slid her arm around Jed's waist, pressing closer to him. "He missed his daddy. And so did his mommy."

For a moment, their eyes connected, and he saw the pain she tried to hide, and all the worry, too.

"How are you feeling, son?" Rodney rested his hands on Becky's shoulders. They both stood in front of Jed.

"I'm good, just tired."

Neil patted his shoulder. "You look a little pale. You feeling okay?"

"Would everybody please stop? If I'm pale, it's because I've been stuffed in some hospital bed with no sun."

"Hey, Jed. Glad you're back," Andy shouted from the corral.

"Thanks, Andy." He looked back at his dad and then Brad. "So what's with the roof and all the workers? What's going on?"

He gazed down on Diana, who seemed to stiffen. Her round cheeks pinkened, and she licked her lips. "Jed, don't be mad."

He wasn't mad—he was annoyed because everyone kept sticking their noses in his business, and he'd had enough. "What is it with you guys? You don't think I can look after my family?"

"Jed, come in and have lunch. Everyone, come on in. Then, after we eat, we'll discuss this." Becky reached for Danny and then gave a meaningful glance to Diana, who was still nestled beside Jed.

Diana rested her palm on his chest. "Jed, your mom's right. This can wait." She nudged him until he relented.

He let out a heavy sigh. "Fine."

Rodney and Brad followed.

"Neil, go tell Andy to come in and have lunch with us. I have some sandwiches for his men, too." Becky had a way of organizing everyone and of soothing ruffled feathers, namely Jed's.

Jed was seated at the kitchen table, a plate of sandwiches at the center.

"Jed, do you want coffee?" Diana filled a plate for him, and she watched him anxiously.

"Diana, stop fussing over me. Come here." He held out his hand. He didn't care that his cousin, two brothers and parents were there hovering.

She hesitated for an instant, then strode around the table, put her hand in his. Jed slid back his chair, and she perched on his lap.

"Stop waiting on me. You're looking tired. There's dark circles under your eyes. You been sleeping, seen the doctor yet?" he asked.

"What doctor? Why does Diana need to see a doctor?" Andy asked as he stood on the other side of the table, holding a ham sandwich, and then took a bite, shoving nearly half the sandwich in his mouth.

Neil, looking rather un-Neil-like, dressed in Jed's old t-shirt and faded, ripped-at-the-knees blue jeans, and appearing a little scruffy, as if he hadn't shaved for a day or two, took a large bite of his own sandwich as he strode beside Andy and slung his arm around his shoulder. "It appears my little brother has gone and gotten his wife knocked up again, which, the proud uncle-to-be that I am, is going to give me another nephew or niece to spoil."

Andy had the oddest expression on his face before taking another bite of his sandwich, and then he said, "Congratulations. That's great news." But he didn't sound all that happy.

Neil grinned that charming, dashing smile that had his whole face lighting up, a smile that drew everyone to him. He was the life of the party, always had been, and Jed knew as he glanced from Neil to Andy that something more was going on.

"Grab another sandwich there, cous, and let's get back to work." Neil slapped Andy on the back.

Andy shook his head. "No, I'm good." He crammed the last bite in his mouth and jabbed a finger toward Jed. "Take it easy for a bit. Glad you're back and on the mend." Then he strode out the door, where Neil waited. Neil's cell phone rang, and he reached in his back pocket and answered it as he strode out the door.

Rodney and Brad sat on the sofa together, each with their own plate, Becky in the rocker. Danny was in his playpen in the corner, jabbering away as he shoved his toys in his mouth and then played with each one.

Jed ran his hand up Diana's back. "You didn't answer me, Diana. How're you feeling?"

"I'm just tired. I'm sure I'll be able to sleep better tonight now that you're home."

Jed reached out and traced the dark circles under her eyes with his thumb, and the tiny lines around her eyes appeared to deepen. Jed pulled her hair loose from the ponytail she'd bound it in.

"Jed, no, I can't work with it hanging in my face."

"Leave it. I love it." He ran his fingers through her deep red locks, which drifted past her shoulders in waves almost down to her waist.

A throat cleared behind him. Jed dropped his hand and stared at Brad, who helped himself to another sandwich. "Do you have time to talk?"

Diana scooted off Jed's knee. "Go talk to your brother, Brad. I'm going to get Danny changed and cleaned up."

Jed watched his wife's derriere, which sweetly filled out her tan capris as she bent over and picked up their son. Before she walked away, she gestured sharply with her head toward Brad, and Jed felt three pairs of eyes burning into him.

CHAPTER

Thirteen

"Well, who's first? Dad, Mom, Brad?" Jed glanced at each of them, and they looked at each other.

Jed crossed his arms. His back was beginning to ache from sitting up for so long, and after the long ride home from the hospital. He pushed away, stood up, and swayed.

"Are you okay?" Brad grabbed his arm.

"Yeah, just stood up too fast." Jed steadied himself against the edge of the table.

"Jed, come sit on the sofa. Put your feet up." Rodney hovered on the other side of Jed. Becky glanced down the hall to Danny's room, a flash of worry set on her round, motherly face.

"Don't, Mom. Don't start worrying Diana."

Becky firmed her lips and gave Jed another hard, motherly glance. "Sit down on the sofa, Jed. You probably shouldn't be out of the hospital yet."

Jed let his mother fuss as his brother walked him over.

When he was settled, the dizziness passed, but his family still hovered. "Sit down. You're all making me nervous."

Rodney and Becky sat on the loveseat, and Brad took the rocker.

"So how much are these workers here costing me?" Jed snapped.

"Jed, it's costing you nothing. Andy brought them. They're his people," Brad said.

"So does Andy know my financial problems, too?" Jed asked, watching the three glance at each other.

Rodney cleared his throat. "No, son. He offered to bring his people over—"

"*I* suggested he help. You know, like a community barn raising." Neil now hovered in the open doorway, then closed the front door behind him. "Jed, this is family business, which is us. Andy's our cousin, and there are some things that aren't shared and stay between us. I'm smart enough to know that."

Jed watched Neil, appreciating his dynamic older brother, who was the clown of the family. He never realized how much Neil understood his feelings. "Well, thank you for that, at least."

"You're welcome. Oh, but I did go ahead and pay for everything, including modifying your covered area to include a heated inside viewing area to keep overstressed parents dry, happy, and out of the way." Neil flashed a smile, showing his white, straight teeth.

Jed noticed his mother was worrying about how he'd respond to that.

"Redesigned, huh? Please tell me you haven't included some four-star fancy upgrade that is absolutely useless." Jed smiled at Neil.

"Hell, no. Just some necessities: coffee and tea station for the parents, some comfortable chairs to sit in. And you'll be happy to know they're just cheap cloth, not the leather ones."

"Well, thanks for that. I suppose you're not going to tell me how much everything came to or let me pay you back?" Jed asked.

Becky gasped, and Rodney and Brad shared a glance.

"We thought you'd be furious," Brad said.

Neil winked at his brother. "I told you he was softening."

"This is for Diana. So… thank you." Jed watched his dad and Brad stare at him and wondered if they were about to call the doctor and ask what happened to their son.

"Just don't go spending any more money. We don't need fancy. Just doable," Jed added.

"Son, I wanted to talk with you about the bank." Rodney leaned forward, clasping his hands between his legs.

"I'll call the bank, take care of them. I don't need—"

His father interrupted. "Son, I paid off the mortgage."

The only thing that could be heard was the squeak of the rocker in Danny's room as everyone waited for Jed's response.

"Now, Jed, don't be mad. I want you to understand I've never been so proud as I sit back and watch you do all this on your own—"

"Oh, Dad, stop, please," Neil interrupted again. "Jed, we all had a family meeting. Brad, Dad and me. Mom told us we had to talk to you first. Sorry, Mom. We didn't listen to you."

Diana stood in the hallway just outside the living room, watching. Jed saw her hesitation. He held out his hand. "Diana, is Danny asleep?"

"Yeah." She strode over to Jed and sat beside him,

linking her fingers with his. The softness in her vivid blue eyes, the way she leaned closer to him, squeezing his hand, he knew she was uncomfortable.

"Neil was just telling me about the family meeting." Jed watched his wife and the frown that formed between her brows.

"Jed, your family is just trying to help," Diana said. "We should talk about this."

"Don't come down on Diana, Jed. We actually didn't ask her, either. She has enough stress and worry," Brad interrupted. "If you're angry at someone, then pick me."

"No one is going to be mad at anyone," Becky said. "It's done. And there's one thing, Jed, you may not be aware. Each of you boys was left property or money. Jed, you may not realize, but each of you boys has something set aside from your granddaddy. You may have decided to walk away, but that money is still yours. What were we supposed to do with it? Throw it in the street? Yes, you've shown everyone, this entire family, that you can do it on your own, you stubborn kid. But I stuck what was yours into a trust in your name." Becky stood up and strode to the kitchen chair, which her purse was slung over. She reached in and pulled out an envelope and walked back over to Jed. Everyone watched her.

"Here." She held out the envelope to Jed. "Take this."

He couldn't help but admire his mom and wonder what she'd gone and done. He hesitated and then took the envelope, opening it and pulling out the papers inside. He unfolded them, and Diana gasped as she pressed against him, reading the statements.

"There, it's in your name. I'm not keeping it, and neither is your dad. It's your money. You can save it and pass it on to Danny or give it away." Becky sat beside

Rodney again, and he shook his head, chuckling under his breath.

"Jesus Murphy, Mom, what did you do? There's almost a million dollars in here. What am I supposed to do with all that?" Jed felt beads of sweat dampen the back of his neck, and something warmed in his heart, maybe because everything had changed, and so had his future.

CHAPTER *Fourteen*

"Are you sure you're okay?" Diana hovered, pressing her hand to Jed's forehead as he sat on the edge of their bed.

"I'm fine, Diana. Don't start fretting. I'm just tired." Jed started to unbutton his shirt when Diana swatted his hands away and unbuttoned it for him.

"I'm entitled to worry, and until you're one hundred percent, I will keep worrying that you don't overdo it." She slid his plaid shirt off his broad shoulders, which had paled from the time he spent in the hospital. "You haven't said much about the money, Jed. I didn't expect that from you."

His deep brown eyes held a mystery that seemed more pronounced. Something was different as he looked up at Diana. "I can get you and Danny everything you need." He covered his hand over the softness of her stomach. "And this baby, too. I want to make sure you're looked after."

"What are you talking about? Danny and I have everything we need. You!" Diana tried to step back, but Jed slid his other hand over her hips and then down and pulled her between his legs. She slid her arms gently around his neck. "I love you, Jed. I don't want stuff."

"You don't want nice things? A bigger house, maybe?" Jed asked.

He was strong for a man who'd been flat out in the hospital. He slid his hands up her thin t-shirt and skimmed her breasts with the tips of his fingers. Then pressed his face into her breasts and breathed in her scent.

Diana felt everything inside her warm. Being touched by Jed scattered her reasonable mind. She couldn't think. She pressed her lips to the top of his head, ran her fingers through his wavy brown hair, which still needed cutting.

Jed skimmed his fingers down to her waistband and undid the button, slid the zipper down.

"Jed, we can't. You just got home…." Diana didn't want him to stop, though, not really.

"Yes, we can, carefully. I want you so much." He hooked his hands in the waistband of her underwear and slid them down with her pants until they pooled at her feet. "Step out." Then he pulled her with him as he lay back on the bed. Pressing his hand to the back of her head, he kissed her as if he was a drowning man and she was his last breath. Fiercely, possessively, his tongue touched and teased hers. He deepened the kiss as he slid his hand under her shirt, up her back, and unhooked her bra, breaking the kiss away to lift it off and toss it on the floor.

Diana's hand shook as she unhooked his belt. "Lift up."

Jed watched her with hooded eyes, lifting his hips so she could pull off his jeans, underwear, and socks. She touched him gently, curiously. He was ready, and she didn't want to wait. She missed him and needed him inside of her now.

Diana lowered herself onto him, her palms on his

nicely formed chest, with the light brown chest hair she smoothed with her fingertips as she sank down onto him.

Jed gripped her hips as she set her rhythm, controlling her depth, deep and slow, and then pulled her forward as she moved, tasting her lush red lips, kissing her deeply.

"Jed, you feel so good. Oh, lord, I missed you. I need you," Diana whispered as she sat up, moving slowly and deeply. Jed ran his hands over her creamy white stomach and the tiny stretch marks left from Danny. He traced the underside of her perfectly round breast, which Danny still nursed from. He ran circles around her nipples and watched her eyes flare with passion as she rose up, ran her hands through her hair, tilting her head back. She shut her eyes.

"Oh, Jed," she whispered as he ran his hands around her breasts and felt that magic pull that would take her to completion.

Lost in wave after wave, she heard him grunt when she slowed and he gripped her hips, moving her until he too joined her.

Diana lay sprawled across his chest, her eyes closed. He was still inside her. His large, rough hands skimmed her back in light circles and then down, running possessively over her derriere.

"Did I hurt you?" she whispered.

His chest rumbled, and she started to pull away to sit up, but Jed tightened his hold and pressed a kiss to the top her head, laughing softly. "God, woman, you feel too damn good."

"Jed, let me move off you. I don't want to hurt you," Diana whispered.

He helped her slide off and move beside him, his arm snaked around her, holding her to his side. He pulled the old green comforter around her shoulders

"I think I might be able to sleep tonight." She slid her cheek against his shoulder and peered up at him.

Jed looked down on her, the light from the beside lamp illuminating the cluttered tiny bedroom. "You haven't been sleeping?"

"Not without you. I never realized how safe you make me feel. The thought of you not being there… of me losing you…" Her throat ached, and she had to stop as she squeezed her eyes shut. "I don't ever want to go through that again."

She felt Jed's arms tighten around her. "Honey. I'm here with you now."

Diana tilted her face up and touched Jed's lips with hers, a kiss that was so tender, so soft, where she opened herself to the man she loved.

"Go to sleep," he whispered against her forehead. He could feel his wife relax, her breathing evening out. Jed lay there, again thinking it was better not to tell her. It was better she had some peace now for her and the baby, but that by no means stopped that little voice from dousing him with guilt. He had sworn to love, honor, and protect his wife, till death do them part, and it rang over and over in his head.

CHAPTER *Fifteen*

"Jed, do you want some breakfast?" Diana asked as Jed strode into the tiny kitchen, his hair sticking up, still barefoot in his blue jeans as he buttoned up his shirt.

"Yeah, I can do it." He leaned down and kissed Diana slowly, thoughtfully, a proper good-morning kiss to his wife.

"No, sit down. I'll put some eggs on for you."

"Can't argue with that." Jed stumbled and braced his hand on the wall.

"Jed, are you okay?" Diana gripped his arm and slid her other around his waist. "I'm calling the doctor."

Footsteps clomped up the front steps. The door opened. "What's going on?" Brad didn't hesitate as he lunged forward and grabbed Jed's other arm, pulled out a kitchen chair. "Sit down."

"He lost his balance," Diana shrieked. "I'm calling the doctor."

"S—s—stop," Jed stuttered.

Diana gazed down into Jed's face. His eyes seemed glossy and distant. "Brad, something's wrong."

Brad yanked out his cell phone.

"Who are you calling?" asked Diana. She met the hard set of Brad's jaw.

"An ambulance."

"Stop it, both of you. Brad, hang up that phone," Jed muttered, his voice clearer. His brows furrowed with irritation.

Brad disconnected. "Hey, look, you're not okay. What happened there, Jed?" He rested his palm on the table and leaned down in front of his brother.

"I just turned around too fast. That's all. Diana, I thought you were going to make me breakfast. I'm starving." He flashed Diana one of his crooked grins.

She couldn't believe it. "I'll make you breakfast, and then I'm calling the doctor." Diana hesitated and then grabbed a frying pan, cracked two eggs in it, and just happened to catch a glimpse of something that passed between Jed and Brad.

"What's going on with you two?" She scrambled the eggs in the pan with a fork, listened to them sizzle, and set two pieces of bread in the toaster.

"Everything's fine, Diana." Jed didn't look at her when he said it. In fact, he stared at Brad, who said nothing but stared right back at Jed with that same hard suspicious glance all the Friessen men seemed to possess.

Diana dished up the eggs, buttered the toast, and set it all before Jed. "Now I'm calling the doctor." She reached for the phone, and Jed reached for her, but she yanked her arm away and glared first at Brad, then Jed. "I'm calling the doctor now, and you're not stopping me."

Maybe it was the determination that blazed like a torch heating her blood. Her face heated, and both Brad and Jed appeared to back up, even though they hadn't moved.

"Jed, if I were you, I'd let your wife call the doctor, or

I'll have to hose both of us down from the fire she's about to set on us," Brad said as he rested a hand on Jed's shoulder.

Jed merely grunted and shoved a forkful of eggs into his mouth.

Diana yanked a business card from the corkboard nailed to the dining room wall, where she pinned every important paper, notice, and business card.

She dialed the number.

"Doctor Hardy's office."

"This is Diana Friessen. Is Doctor Hardy available?" She stared at Jed, who was eating and watching her with those dark-rimmed eyes, brighter than earlier. She wondered if she was making something out of nothing.

Music blared on the phone when she was put on hold. Then a deep voice came on the line. "Diana, this is Doctor Hardy. Is everything all right?"

"Well, that's actually why I'm calling. Jed nearly keeled over. He lost his balance. He said he just moved too fast."

"I see. Is your husband there?"

Diana held the phone out, stared at the receiver, and then pressed it to her ear. "Yes, he's right here."

"Can I talk to him?"

Diana was puzzled, and her sharp lawyer's mind suddenly blanked. "Okay."

She held out the phone to Jed. "Doctor Hardy wants to talk to you."

Jed reached for the phone as if it was nothing. "Hello." Then he smiled. "No, no, everything's fine.... Hmm, yes, I understand."

Diana wanted to jump up and down and scream at this one-sided conversation. She wished at this point that they had one of those fancy phones with the speaker so she could hear, too. She glanced at Brad. He shrugged.

"Yup, I understand...." Jed sighed and then hung up, dumping the phone on the table.

"Well... what did the doctor say?" Diana barked and slapped the table in front of his plate.

"He told me to take it easy. Great eggs by the way, Diana." He shoved the plate away and leaned his elbows on the table.

"Doesn't he want to see you? Examine you?" Diana darted her frustrated gaze to Brad and back to Jed.

"Expect a visit later today. That make you happy?"

Diana let out a frustrated sigh and ground her teeth. "Yes, it does."

IT WAS three hours exactly from the time Jed hung up the phone to the time that a black sedan was spotted. A trail of dust followed what Diana could clearly see was a Lexus as it pulled in and parked in the parking lot Jed had carved out in front of the barn.

Workers were hammering and bustling around the riding ring, working on the additions that Neil had designed. Becky and Rodney had gone into town with Danny to pick up some groceries. Diana crossed her arms and stiffened when a hard, muscled arm slung over her shoulders. She relaxed when she realized it was Brad, but when she glanced back at the Lexus and the person who stepped out, she stiffened again.

"Hello, Diana. Is Jed around?"

What the hell was Doctor Gordon doing here? The woman was taller than Diana, slim, curvy, and she had long, dark hair that fell in waves. She was dressed in a gray pantsuit with a matching tank top, and she was gorgeous.

"Jed's resting in the house." It was Brad who spoke,

because Diana was struggling to suppress the growl that was her first response to this clingy woman.

"Where's Doctor Hardy?" Diana finally found her voice, but she realized too late that she sounded rude and shrewish.

Brad must have known, as he squeezed Diana's shoulder.

Doctor Gordon's smile faltered. She cleared her throat, then reached in the backseat of her car and lifted a small backpack and slung it over her shoulder. "Doctor Hardy couldn't make it. But we were concerned from your call. I was coming out this way anyway—"

Diana cut her off. "So you thought you'd drop by and check on my husband."

Doctor Gordon froze as if she'd been struck.

Ouch. Diana immediately regretted her remark. Her cheeks burned. "I'm sorry.... That was..."

Doctor Gordon opened her mouth to say something.

"Come inside, doc." Brad still held Diana but swept his hand welcomingly toward the house.

Diana wanted to hide, but she couldn't. She glanced up at Brad, and he watched her, sharing her awkwardness as he ran his hand over his short, dark hair.

"Thank you. So tell me, what exactly happened this morning?"

Diana cleared her throat. "He turned to go sit at the table, and he lost his balance and staggered and grabbed the wall." Diana and Brad kept pace with the doctor. Brad dropped his arm as they strode up the plain box steps that were still missing a hand railing. The woman didn't even flinch or bat an eye as she followed Brad, Diana bringing up the rear.

By the time Diana stepped into the house, Jed was in the living room, sitting on the sofa. Doctor Gordon set her backpack beside him and unzipped it. "So what happened this morning, Jed?"

"Diana's making too much of it. I just turned too fast, is all."

Diana closed the door and leaned against it, watching the doctor pull out her stethoscope, and after she had Jed roll up his sleeve, she fastened a cuff around the hard muscle of his forearm. She pumped it up. "And how are you feeling now? Any dizziness?"

"No, I'm fine," he said. "Had a nap because my wife insisted."

Diana crossed her arms, feeling a wave of unease she hadn't felt in a long time. She knew it had a lot to do with the woman here now with her back to Diana, in her house, touching her husband. She also knew Brad was watching her from across the room. She could feel his heat, his watchfulness, but Diana wouldn't look over.

"Well, blood pressure is good." Doctor Gordon ripped off the black cuff, then used an electronic ear thermometer to take Jed's temperature. "Temperature's good."

"Doc, gotta tell you this is a wasted trip out here for you."

Her back still to Diana, the doctor glanced up at Brad. "Would you mind stepping out for a minute so I can examine Jed and speak with him, too, for just a minute?"

Diana felt her back stiffen because, for one, the woman didn't address her as Jed's wife. Damn the woman to hell—she was crossing some serious boundaries. How dare she ask her to leave her own house?

Brad cleared his throat and said, "Yeah, sure," and tapped Jed on the shoulder. With a glance, he gestured toward Diana, planted against the door, the spot she had no intention of moving one step from.

"Diana..." Jed started to say.

"No, Jed. I'm your wife. I'm not leaving, and if she wants to examine you, she does it in front of me. You think I'm walking out the door and leaving you with this woman who I walked in on fawning herself all over you like some tart?" Diana shouted. She was shaking so hard.

"Diana, enough," Jed barked.

The doctor stiffened and then tossed her items back in the backpack.

Jed's dark eyes singled Diana out from across the room and narrowed. His lips thinned, pressed hard together, and she knew she'd hit a nerve. She flattened her hand over her mouth, ashamed, mortified for what she'd said, even though she meant every word.

"Jed, your wife deserves to know," Doctor Gordon stated.

"Know what? What's going on, Jed?" Diana asked, feeling as if she was the odd man out. This time, she closely watched the silent communication that passed between her husband and the gorgeous woman with mile-long legs. Doctor Gordon turned so Diana could see her profile, and she tucked a stray lock of dark hair behind her ears. Her mouth tightened, and she had a face with cheekbones a cover model would kill for. Diana looked up at Brad, who was also staring down at Jed.

And Jed, the stubborn lout, was watching the attractive doctor.

Diana didn't think. She just yanked the door open and stepped out, slamming it behind her and stumbling down the wooden steps on legs that felt like all the starch had been washed out of them. She had no idea where she was going. Cars, trucks were parked here and there in front of the barn and house. A half dozen men hired to finish the arena, which was supposed to have been a simple corral, hammered and constructed the roof, but the hammering barely registered. She heard her name called as she walked into the barn, grabbed a halter from a hook just inside, and marched to the gated pasture where the horses were grazing. She unlatched the gate and closed it, seeking out Scarlett, her dark mare. The horse must have picked up her scent, because she nickered and picked her way across the field, toward Diana.

"Scarlet, come here, girl." Diana strode to her horse and slipped the halter on. She clucked her tongue and led her to the gate, where Andy, dressed in a dark t-shirt, with his short, dark hair groomed impeccably, leaned and watched her. Although the family resemblance to Jed was uncanny, they were so different.

Andy unlatched the gate and closed it after her. He didn't say a word as he matched her stride to where she tied Scarlett outside the barn.

Diana didn't look up as she grabbed a tack box and set it on the ground in easy reach. She used the curry comb on Scarlett, scrubbing circles in the thick dark hair that was coming out in clumps as her winter coat was beginning to shed.

Andy stayed on the other side of Scarlett, resting his arm on the mare's back, watching Diana. "You okay?"

She hesitated, and her breathing faltered when she glimpsed something in the dark blue of his eyes: concern, caring, protectiveness? But she had no desire to tread anywhere down that path. "I'm fine." Even to her, she didn't sound convincing.

"You don't look fine." Andy inclined his head toward the house. "Heard the doctor is here. Jed okay?"

She must have really dug in with the comb, as Scarlett flinched. "Sorry, girl." She rubbed the spot with her hand and gentled her motions. "Honestly, I don't really know.

Seems I'm to be kept in the dark about something," she snapped.

"What do you mean?"

Diana grabbed a brush and brushed Scarlett. Andy stepped back and moved with Diana as she groomed the other side. "He was dizzy, said he just moved too fast. But when I looked in his eyes, Andy, there was something not quite right. He had this faraway look. I can't explain it.... It scared me. And that doctor..." Diana couldn't force herself to repeat her name, as it burned like bitters on her tongue. "She knows *something*, and only she and Jed are in on it. What is it with these damn secrets?" She had to clear her throat, as her voice wavered. She grabbed a hoof pick and dug out the mud embedded in each of Scarlett's hooves.

Andy said nothing. He gazed at the house, then back at her. She could tell he was thinking something and wondered for a moment if he was going in to speak with Jed. Diana caught a glimpse of the house and realized Brad was still inside. Maybe Jed had decided to confide in him, at least, but that didn't lessen the ache of loneliness. Her husband may have been there, but when he took to sharing secrets with another woman, she didn't and couldn't ignore that. Diana shoved her hands in a bucket of cold water and washed the mud off. She dried them on her jeans and walked into the barn, grabbing the horse blanket and tossing it on Scarlett's back. When she started to lift the worn dark saddle from the peg in the small tack room, Andy was right there and snatched it from her.

"What are you doing?"

She reached for the saddle, but he held tight, and there was no way she'd be able to pry it from his hands. "Andy, give me the saddle."

He shook his head. "You're not getting on the horse, Diana. Didn't you just find out you're pregnant again?"

"Oh, for God's sake, Andy, I'm not that far along. It's perfectly safe. I rode Scarlett through my pregnancy with Danny."

His eyes flared a darker blue. "Mm hmm. And you went into early labor while riding and were sent by ambulance to the hospital, where you had an emergency C-section."

"Oh, Andy, that was from the stress of Jed's accident. My God, when we found him with a broken leg, bleeding… I'm not surprised I didn't go into labor right then and there." She tried to pull the saddle from Andy again, but she couldn't budge him.

"Fine, you keep the saddle. I'll ride bareback." She dug into each step back to Scarlett, her hand on the blanket, ready to yank it off, when Andy sat the saddle overtop. She stared for a minute at the hard set of his face as he snatched a second halter off the rack of hooks.

"Well, you're not going riding alone." He strode away, muttering under his breath, "Damn stubborn woman, you are."

She couldn't help the ache that settled in her heart. It should have been Jed here now, not Andy. "Stop it." It didn't matter, she tried to tell herself, but as she finished saddling Scarlett, she couldn't erase the image of that hussy draping herself over her husband, and Jed never once pushing her away.

CHAPTER Sixteen

Diana gave Scarlett her lead as they picked their way through an open sunny trail, which was surrounded by thick brush just sprouting spring leaves, and opened into a large, grassy meadow. Andy was riding one of the newer horses, Pegasus, a pure white Arabian who spooked on a dime. Diana swore she'd never ride her. The horse not only made her extremely nervous but had taken an immediate dislike to her. Except Jed, being Jed, said there was something about Pegasus that made her special, along with the fact that something in his gut just felt right. It helped too that the price was right, since her previous owner couldn't get a saddle on her. Pegasus was a spirited horse that spooked at everything and was impossible to trailer—well, for Diana, anyway. However, Andy, just like Jed, had no trouble with his seat and had somehow calmed the horse.

"What's really got you so upset, Diana?" Andy reined Pegasus up next to Scarlett.

"My husband has shut me out. First he doesn't tell me

about how far in debt we are, and the grant was pulled for the horse center. And now this doctor and Jed—"

"What do you mean the grant was pulled?" Andy snapped, reaching over as he yanked on Diana's reins, pulling Scarlett to a stop.

Diana sputtered. "Andy… what are you doing?" She tried to yank her reins back, but the firm set of his jaw and a flash of anger from him had her resting her hands on the saddle horn.

"Andy, the grant we were supposed to have for the therapeutic equine center would have covered the necessary upgrades, our start-up costs, and all the equipment we needed. Apparently, the state cut funding for all special needs. Jed said nothing to me. He just kept it all to himself. That's why he was so stressed, and tired, and now I know why we're so broke."

Andy looked away. His jaw slackened as if he were confused. "Diana, are you sure that's what they said, funding cuts?"

"Andy, Jed got a letter from the state, and that's what he told me."

"Who sent him the letter?"

The way Andy kept asking, Diana had a sinking feeling that something wasn't quite right.

"I don't know. Why?"

He adjusted his hat and handed back the reins. "Let's go. I want to have a talk with Jed."

"No more. I'm sorry, Andy, but I have been kept in the dark for the last time. You want to talk to Jed, fine, but you talk to me, too, now." Scarlett picked that moment to step back and away from Pegasus. "Whoa, girl, it's okay."

"Do you remember when Laura's son was taken from her, and what it took to get him back? The senator and my parents were trying to get me to marry Alexis. Well, threats were made by my mother that unless I married Alexis, she'd see to it that Jed's funding for the center was pulled. She knew how much I cared for Jed, and hurting him would be a way to keep me in line."

"Are you telling me that your mother is responsible for this?" Diana asked, stamping down the urge to yell and scream. "My husband was almost killed, and she may be responsible. What the hell is wrong with that woman, Andy?"

"Diana, the only thing Caroline has ever been concerned with is what's best for Caroline. So you really need to ask that?" Andy pulled his horse around and walked her back a few steps. "Look, I don't even know for sure it was her, but I mean to find out. Let's head back."

Diana gazed ahead at the trail that led up to the old logging road, not wanting to go back just yet to face the doctor, to face Jed. She was still hurting, and that sense of being cut out of the life of the one person who meant everything to her was like a stinger just under her skin that she couldn't pick out.

"Diana … forget it. We're going back." He moved Pegasus in front of her.

"Andy, I want you to promise me something."

He stared at her with his steel blue eyes. His face, for all the emotion it showed, could have been made of granite. He appeared to consider something before nodding once. "All right."

"Whatever you find out about the state funding, if Caroline was responsible for having it pulled or not, I want to know everything, and I want you to tell me." She hoped and held her breath for a second before he nodded again.

"I'm going to have to tell Jed, too. He may not want you to know."

"What is it with you Friessen men, wanting to hide

everything? If you think keeping all this a secret is helping and protecting me, well, you're wrong."

"Diana, I understand why Jed's doing this. Can't say I'd do it any different." Andy chirped, and Pegasus started back the way they came.

"So how does Laura feel about you hiding things from her?"

He didn't answer, and Diana stared at the solid wall of the first Friessen man to turn her life upside down. She wondered about Laura, how she was doing. Maybe she'd call her, ask her to come out and find out what was going on. After all, these Friessen men could be a handful, infuriating and secretive. Laura, being young and inexperienced, may have needed a friendly ear and someone to talk to. But first, Diana had her own secretive man to deal with.

CHAPTER Seventeen

"You need to tell her." Brad shoved his hands in his jeans pocket and stood beside Jed at the bottom of the front steps. "I need to call Emily, too."

"You should call your wife, but you should go home too, Brad. Appreciate all you've done, but I'm sure Emily needs you home." Jed stared up the road at the retreating taillights of Margaret Gordon's car. She was an intriguing woman who reminded him so much of his wife's own passion and dedication to a cause. They both gave all of themselves to anything they took on. He didn't know what made him look, but he spied two riders coming in from the north trail. As he looked closer, he realized it was Andy riding that pure white Arabian he'd bought. He straightened his stance when he caught a glimpse of Scarlett and his wife, Diana, riding her.

"What the hell is she doing on a horse?" He started toward the barn, ready to lay into her—and that cousin of his, for taking her out to begin with.

He staggered a bit.

Brad grabbed his arm. "Whoa, take a breath. I think

I'll call that doc to get back here or haul you back to Seattle myself."

Jed pressed his fingers into his forehead as a wave dizziness finally passed. "I'm fine. Just moved too fast, is all. And I made my decision. I told you and that doctor, too."

"Jed, if you don't tell Diana, I will. You're not being fair to her. This is her decision, too. She's your wife." Brad dropped his hand. "And you need to tell Mom and Dad. Neil, too. We're family, Jed."

Jed glanced at his brother and into his solemn eyes, and before he could allow his brother's feelings to affect him, Jed started toward the barn, where both horses were now tied and Andy and Diana had both dismounted. Diana saw him coming, and her deep blue eyes widened right before she pursed her lush, kissable lips.

"What the hell are you doing, taking my wife out riding a horse? She's pregnant. I don't want her on a horse, period. Have you forgotten what happened last time?" Jed felt the fury snap in his words, and he had to fight the urge not to plant his fist in Andy's face, because right now, Andy was crossing lines that he had no business treading.

"Jed, stop it. It's not Andy's fault. He only went with me because I wouldn't listen to him, because he sounded just like you do now." Diana ran her hand over Scarlett's flank and took a few steps closer to Jed. Then she stopped, placing her hand on her hip. Her t-shirt clung to her full breasts, and her shapely hips were outlined nicely in her faded jeans.

"Jed, you're right. She shouldn't have been on a horse." Andy held up his hands, and Diana glared at him as if she wanted to kick him.

"Well, both of you, as far as I'm concerned, can take your cave-man attitudes and shove them. I'm *done* with it, Jed, with you protecting me and keeping me out of the loop." Diana yanked on the leather buckle and unfastened the saddle. "And then you decided to confide in some other woman and not me, your wife, and you let her dismiss me from my own house. I'm done with all your secrets," she shouted, then started to yank off the saddle and horse blanket.

Jed stepped forward. "Don't you dare lift that saddle."

But it was Brad who calmly stepped in and took it from her. "Diana, you and your husband have some things to talk about." He turned to Andy. "Andy, I'll help you with the horses."

Jed stared at his wife, who stood just outside his reach. Her arms hung loosely at her sides, and her long red hair hung in her face. A beautiful sight, even when her eyes were spitting fire as if to roast him alive.

"What do you have to tell me, Jed? That you need your brother to tell you to talk to me? Oh, wait. Your lady friend, the doctor—let me guess, she already knows, too."

Holy crap, he'd need a pair of tweezers to yank out the stinger from that sharp remark. "Diana, let's go inside." He held out his hand, but instead of taking it, she crossed her arms and stepped around him, stomping away toward the house.

Jed glanced at his brother, who winced, and at Andy, who looked rightly confused, squinting at Diana's retreating backside and then at Jed.

"When you're done talking to your wife, I need to have a word with you about that grant," Andy said.

Jed couldn't think about the grant, and at the moment, that was the least of his concerns. Brad was right. He did need to tell Diana, and he couldn't bear to see the look in her eyes when all he wanted to do was protect her and keep her safe, but what he had to say would crush her.

CHAPTER *Eighteen*

"Do you want some coffee, something to eat?" She didn't know what to do or how to be here with Jed right now. She couldn't shake the sense of betrayal. She yanked open the fridge and pulled out the leftover chicken from last night's dinner, setting it on the counter with tomatoes and lettuce. Jed stepped behind her and slid both arms around her waist, pressing his hand possessively over her stomach. She leaned back almost on instinct. She was mad, but she couldn't fight his touch. She rested her head against his shoulder, and Jed pressed his rough cheek against hers.

"You need to shave." She reached up and ran her hand over the light hair that was so much like sandpaper after a few days of not shaving.

"I don't want you on a horse anymore, Diana, not when you're pregnant. It's too dangerous." He held her tight, and when she tried to turn around, he kissed her cheek. "I love you, and no matter how calm Scarlett is, the fact is, Diana, horses spook. You could get thrown, and you could lose the baby. Our baby."

She managed to turn in his arms and placed her hands on his shoulders, gazing into his amber brown eyes, which never failed to take her breath away. "Jed, I'm careful. I'm just walking her. I'm not taking chances—"

"Diana, please. I'm asking you to stay off. With Danny, that scared the life out of me. After the baby, you can get back on. I'm sorry, but it has to be that way."

She didn't want to keep arguing about it, because deep down she knew he was right. With what had just happened to Jed, she almost lost him. "Okay. Now I want to know what you've been hiding from me. No more secrets, Jed."

He looked away over her head as if deciding what he should say. She pushed against his chest and wiggled free from his arms, stepping out of the small kitchen, and then faced Jed, wanting to yell and scream and make him tell her everything. "Does she know?"

For a minute, Jed looked confused, and he glanced at the door when Diana jabbed her finger. "Who?"

"That tart of a doctor who was draped all over you, the one with her arm around you when I walked into your hospital room to pick you up, and you let her. You never pushed her away. And then today, for some reason, she shows up here and not Doctor Hardy, who, by the way, in case you've forgotten, is your doctor. Just what the hell was she doing here, anyway? Why is she so interested in you? Something you share together? Tell me, please, because I really want to know!"

Jed took two steps toward her and pressed his hands on her shoulders to hold her still. "Stop, Diana. It's not like that." He turned her toward the sofa. "I need to sit down."

She looked up into his pale face, and her anger was forgotten. "Jed, are you okay?" She wrapped her arm around his waist and guided him to the sofa. He sat and pulled her down with him.

"I'm fine." He leaned back and shut his eyes for a second. Color returned to his face, and he opened his eyes and reached for her hand. Then he laughed at her.

"I've never known you to be jealous. A tart of a doctor? Come on, Diana. She's a nice lady."

Diana tried to yank her hand away, but Jed held tight.

"Diana, she reminds me of you, taking on a cause, caring."

She wanted to hit him and felt her spine straightening as if someone had stuck a rod against it and tied her to it. Her face warmed. "If you ask me, she *cares* a little too much. You're my husband, or have you forgotten?"

Jed raised his eyebrows and then tried to hide his smile. "No, I'd never forget who I've given my heart to."

Well, that stopped her. How would she respond to that? She opened her mouth but couldn't find one intelligent word, and he pulled her hand to his mouth and pressed a kiss into the back of her hand.

"There is something I need to talk to you about." Jed laced his fingers with hers and rested them on his lap. "The doctors did a brain scan and found something."

Diana stared at something in her husband's eyes that she hadn't seen before, and she felt a bone-chilling numbness that brought on a fear she hadn't felt in a very long time. "Jed..." She couldn't finish, as tears blurred her eyes.

"Diana, they found a shadow in part of my brain. They said it's a tumor...."

"What do you mean? A brain tumor, cancer?"

"Diana, they don't know if it's cancer. It's just a shadow...."

"What do you mean, a shadow? Well, they'll go in get it out, and then we'll deal with it. When do they want to operate?"

Jed gripped both her hands, which were trembling. "They can't go in."

"Of course they can go in. They do it all the time." She touched his chest, gripped his cotton shirt.

"Diana, it's in a part of the brain they can't operate on. If they tried, I'd be a vegetable, and I won't do that to you."

She didn't know what to say, and she turned and stood at the sound of car doors shutting. The front door opened, and Grandma Becky walked in, carrying Danny in her arms, Rodney behind her, a smile on his face for an instant until he looked at her.

"What's wrong?" It was Becky who asked, and Diana could do nothing as she burst into tears.

CHAPTER *Nineteen*

Her husband held her as she cried. He rubbed her back as she pressed her face into his chest, squeezing his shirtfront, and Jed's hand covered hers.

"Ouch, Diana. Ease up—you got my chest hair. It's all right," Jed whispered and kissed her head, brushing back her hair and sliding his large, calloused hand down her back.

"Jed, what's going on?" Becky asked, holding a now whimpering Danny.

Danny reached out his tiny hands to Jed.

Diana sat up and wiped her eyes. Her face felt tight and cracked, and her stomach felt as if someone had shoved a knife in her and gutted away.

Becky handed Danny to his papa. Diana leaned in and kissed Danny's back, sniffing and hiccuping as she struggled to choke back her sobs. Terrifying Danny was the last thing she wanted to do, but it was exactly what she was doing.

"Diana, what's happened? Is it the baby?" Becky stood

right before them, and when Diana glanced up, Neil hovered behind Becky with Rodney. Concern for her was evident in their eyes. But it was Brad, who lingered in the doorway, his hand resting against the doorframe, with a glassy look in his eyes that made it so real. Brad already knew.

"Jed s—said…" She stuttered and had to stop and take a deep breath.

Jed laced his fingers with hers. "I had to tell Diana some news, something the doctors found."

Diana stared at his big, freckled hand and started to compare the size of each freckle, each knuckles, tracing her hand over the faded white line of a scar from a cut last spring.

"What did the doctors find, Jed?" Neil, always so positive, sounded worried, and when Diana looked up, she saw the seriousness in those strong, earth-brown Friessen eyes.

"Jed said they found a shadow in a part of his brain they can't operate on." Diana cleared her throat again.

"What do you mean by a shadow?" It was Rodney who asked, this time, as he rested both hands on Becky's shoulders. Becky covered her mouth with a trembling hand, her eyes wide and filled with the same agony Diana felt.

"A tumor, Dad, and I need to make sure Diana and Danny are looked after."

Neil rubbed his face with both hands and paced in a circle, sharing a look with Brad.

"Jed, that wasn't all the doctor said. You're not telling everything." Brad took a step toward Jed and shoved both hands on his lean hips.

"Brad, that is all there is to it. Cutting into a part of my brain that will leave me a vegetable isn't a choice or even an option," Jed snapped, and Danny patted Jed's face until he hugged him and kissed his cheek again.

Diana stared at the fire that now blazed in Brad's eyes. When she glanced at her husband and then back at Brad, she had a sinking feeling once again that Jed wasn't telling her everything. She slid back and crossed her arms. "Brad, please tell me everything that my husband once again refuses to tell me."

Brad stared at Jed as if the two of them were locked in some battle together, much like the way two warriors would face off. "Jed, tell everyone here what the doctor really said, and this time you better say all of it."

"Brad, I made my decision."

"What do you mean, you made your decision? You're my husband. We make decisions together as husband and wife, or have you forgotten that part?" Diana snapped, and Danny's tiny lip trembled as he stared with wide eyes at his mommy.

"Diana, I already told you there are just some things I won't do to you. You'd hate me, and I could never stand to have you look at me that way. It's not a life, and if I can't look after myself and you and Danny and our baby, then what kind of man does that make me? No…" He shook his head like a stubborn mule that there was no reasoning with.

"You can hate *me* if you want, Jed, but we love you." Brad looked straight at Diana; he'd made up his mind. "Diana, apparently Doctor Gordon and Doctor Hardy have been trying to reason with Jed. There is a procedure that can be done using some high-tech imaging while they operate so the surgeon knows where to cut. So there is hope."

"You've forgotten that the tumor is in the center of my brain, and the chances of stroke, brain damage, and death are very high."

"Without the surgery, we may as well hop out back

now and start digging your grave!" Brad shouted. Danny shrieked.

"Stop it now." Becky reached down and rescued Danny from his father's arms. "Shh, my precious boy." She swayed and pressed his head against her bosom. Her tan silk shirt was now stained with droplets of baby drool. "Brad, Jed, stop this now. We are going to sit down as a family and discuss this. Rodney, you will call Doctor Hardy. I think it's time we meet with this doctor face to face, all of us together, and find out everything. And no, Jed, this time, when it comes to your life, we are not butting out. Something this serious is not just your decision. You have a wife, a baby, and another on the way. How could you keep this from us?" Becky slid her arm around Diana's shoulder and hugged her while still holding Danny.

Jed flinched, and a hint of pink flushed his cheeks. "Mom, look, I understand how you feel, but this is my decision."

"Oh, poop on you. It's not your decision anymore. I'm beginning to think something more serious happened to your brain when you fell off that roof."

Neil actually choked back what Diana thought was a laugh, and Diana, for the first time ever, felt as though someone other than her husband had her back. She had a mother, something she'd always hoped for but never dared to believe was possible.

"Well, brother dear, it looks like Mom has laid down the law, and I, for one, am interested in the real story this doctor has to say." Neil tossed his arm around Brad's shoulder and then smiled that deep, charming smile at Diana. "Diana, don't you worry, honey. You're not alone in this."

CHAPTER *Twenty*

"Doctor Hardy, thank you so much for meeting on such short notice." Rodney shook the tall, gray-haired doctor's hand. Doctor Hardy flashed warm, caring eyes at Diana, who sat next to her husband in a cozy hospital conference room with a stuffed bookshelf on one wall. Brad and Neil pulled out chairs directly across from Diana and Jed. Brad laced his fingers together and thumped his hand on the table.

Diana realized as she watched the brothers together that they just didn't fit here. They were tall, rugged, hunky cowboys, and as serious as this situation was, she almost smiled to herself, imagining Brad and Jed yanking at their shirt collars as if to breathe. Neil leaned back in the tall chair and winked at Diana. She was sure he could at least trade up the jeans and cowboy gear to a custom-tailored Armani suit and instantly transform himself into boardroom material. Neil had such an amazing smile—his entire face brightened. She wondered if he had anyone special in his life. Diana blinked, then smiled as she realized she was staring. She squeezed Jed's hand, but he was still distracted.

"Well, everyone, have a seat," said Doctor Hardy as he shut the door. Rodney and Becky sat on the other side of Jed, closer to Doctor Hardy, who dropped a file on the table. The doctor rubbed his hands together before leaning on the table. "Jed, glad you have your family here."

Jed nodded. "Yeah, well, as you can see, they didn't give me much choice."

Diana slapped his arm lightly. "Jed."

When he glanced her way, Diana felt something shift in the shaky cocoon Jed had stuffed her in. He was always so strong, so in charge, and it was the strength in his eyes that always grounded her. But not this time, as she sensed fear in him, and that brought the reality of this situation crashing in. Her husband was worried, and this time he couldn't hide it from her. Diana cleared her throat. "Doctor Hardy, we'd like to hear from you the exact details of what you found. And the options."

There was a sharp rap on the door just before it popped open and Margaret Gordon stepped in. Her bright brown eyes softened and connected with Jed's for a second that left no doubt in Diana's mind: The woman cared far too much for Jed. She must have squeezed Jed's hand too hard, as he leaned over and whispered to her, "You can retract your claws now."

Her face heated for a second and she released Jed's hand. "Doctor Hardy, please, if you could fill us in." She ignored Doctor Gordon, who slid out a chair beside Brad. Diana couldn't look at the woman. She'd just as soon shove a handful of nails in her mouth and chew on them than spend a moment in the room with this woman. Why the hell was she here, anyway?

"An image was taken again as a follow-up after surgery, and we discovered a shadow in the center of the brain. We know it's a tumor, and we don't know why it didn't show the first time, but what we do know from the location and type is that this is an aggressive tumor, fast growing, and without treatment, it is fatal."

"Doctor Gordon here has spoken with Jed about options, as well." Doctor Hardy extended a hand to Doctor Gordon, giving her the floor.

Diana leaned back in her chair, stifling the bitterness she felt toward this woman. She didn't want to listen her. Why couldn't Doctor Hardy be in charge and handle this? She couldn't remember the last time she felt such bitterness toward a woman. Every one gave Doctor Gordon their attention, and for the first time, in this room full of family, she felt alone.

"There is a procedure available. By using high-tech imaging techniques, the surgeon is guided and knows exactly where to cut. Only a handful of surgeons are skilled enough to do this, and here at Harborview we also have the equipment needed to perform this technique. Doctor Hardy has performed this procedure numerous times with a high success rate." Doctor Gordon clasped her hands on the table in front of her.

"If it's so successful, why is Jed going on that there are no options and he'll be left a vegetable?" Diana jumped in.

Jed reached over and tried to smooth over her fisted hand. "Diana, they've forgotten to tell you the risks. One slip of the knife or one wrong cut and I'm a vegetable, and that's if I don't stroke out or die on the table."

"Jed, there are always risks with any surgery. But by not taking a chance, you are signing your death warrant. As I said, with this type of tumor, the best case is that you won't live out the year," Doctor Hardy said, as if this was a common conversation he had every day of the week.

"Doctor Hardy, we already know you are one of the

top neurologists in the country. Are there any options other than surgery?" Rodney asked.

"No, and I do welcome you to research other options, talk with other neurologists. Please. Get a second opinion." He faced Rodney and gestured with his flattened hand. "You have the resources, and maybe you should take some time to investigate your options. But I also need to caution you that time is not on your side here. We can treat any symptoms that arise, seizures, and dizziness, with medication. Radiation has sometimes successfully stopped the growth. But this type—"

"What Doctor Hardy is saying is that surgery is Jed's best chance, Mister Friessen." The young, cute doctor addressed Rodney and not Diana. "If I were you, I wouldn't wait. Doctor Hardy is one of the best neurologists in the country, and you'd be making a big mistake letting any other surgeon cut into Jed's head."

"Doctor Hardy, I want you to tell me honestly, from your gut: Can you do this surgery and help my brother?" Brad asked in a deep voice steeped with emotion.

The distinguished doctor exuded confidence and took a measured, controlled breath. He studied everyone seated around the table with a look filled with kindness and not an ounce of hesitation. "Yes."

CHAPTER Twenty-One

Andy Friessen strode into his large mansion, letting the mahogany and glass door slam behind him. The black and white tiles were brightly polished, but he didn't give it a second glance, nor did he acknowledge the maid currently vacuuming the central stairwell that wound its way up to the second floor.

He had a lot on his mind after watching his cousins, Brad, Jed, and Neil, drive out in two vehicles with Rodney, Becky, and Diana for their appointment with the Seattle neurologist. Andy had taken Danny home here with him.

He paused outside the grand library, where his office was, and listened to Danny's babble, which was coming from the kitchen. He sidestepped and ran his hand through his cropped hair. He pushed open the kitchen door, and three pairs of eyes faced him. Laura, his slim, blond wife, was holding Danny and wearing white jeans and a peach t-shirt. Aida, the older cook, and Jules, the head housekeeper, were also there.

"Hi. I didn't know you were home," Laura said. She took a step toward him and paused.

Andy could sense the distance between them and the awkwardness that lingered here in the kitchen with the staff watching, listening. He knew Laura was still friends with Aida, and Jules, well, she had practically raised Andy.

"Where's Gabriel?" Andy asked.

"Your foreman is teaching him to ride that new pony you got him."

She smiled and her face brightened, but there was still awkwardness between them.

Andy reached for Danny. "Come here, you."

Laura hesitated for a second, but Danny held his arms out to his godfather and eagerly went. He cooed and smiled and patted Andy's chest.

"Have you heard from your cousin?" Laura asked, and Aida and Jules stepped closer, listening to every word he said.

"Let's go talk in the library." He said nothing to Aida and Jules, but they took the dismissal well, and Andy pushed open the kitchen door and waited for Laura.

"Jules, can you call me when Gabriel comes in?" Laura asked, as if she expected Jules to say no, as if Jules were still her boss.

Andy realized, as he followed Laura out of the kitchen, that she was still nervous in the house and with the staff. He'd talk to her about that, too.

They stepped into the library, and he glanced around. The maid who had been on the stairs vacuuming was now gone. "Laura, you're my wife now. You don't take orders from Jules and Aida, and you may have been friends before, but you can't be friends with the staff."

She stopped and faced him with a puzzled look. She glanced toward the window and started to say something, but she didn't. She let out a sigh, then finally spoke. "Andy, you undermine me with Jules. You ask her to help me with

Danny as if I'm an incapable twit, which I'm not. You talk to me sometimes like I'm still a servant who works for you. You married me and sleep with me, but you don't share your life with me." She crossed her arms, and he noticed her hand tremble. "And you make me feel sometimes as if I have to answer to her."

Danny pulled up his knees and started bouncing. Drool was dripping from his mouth, and he started gurgling in baby talk. He rubbed his fingers in his mouth and patted wet hands on Andy's dark shirt. Andy smiled and rubbed Danny's bright red hair, stuck when he stared into this baby boy's brilliant blue eyes, his mother's eyes. Andy cleared his throat. "I'm sorry. That was never my intention. I just wanted to—"

"Make sure Diana's baby is looked after by the best." She cut him off, and she watched him with a hardness he hadn't seen before in his very young bride. Her hero worship, he realized, had disappeared as of late.

"No, look, you are capable. I just worry sometimes." The fact was that Diana and he had a past that he swore would connect them till the day they died, and Diana stirred his interest far more than Laura. But he didn't want to hurt her. Hell, he barely knew her. But that wasn't her fault.

"Look, I talked to Neil. They're on their way back and asked if I'd bring Danny home after dinner."

Her face softened. "Andy, how is Jed? What's going on? Did they tell you what the doctor said?"

"No. Neil said we'd talk tonight, that they have some talking to do. I want to be there for my cousin tonight, find out what the doctor said." What he didn't say was that he knew Neil and Brad were keeping him at arm's length. He knew something was going on after that young doctor showed and Jed wasn't feeling well, and the family gathered and left together, asking him to take Danny, with Neil saying they'd talk later. They would talk later. Hell, he was family. Why were they so determined to keep him at arm's length? It was as if every time he was with Diana, Brad and Neil stepped in. He wondered for a minute and then felt the sharp stirring of guilt. He cared for Diana, but he cared for Jed, too.

"I want to come with you tonight," Laura said.

"No, you stay with Gabriel."

Her face flushed, and she flinched as if he had slapped her. She raised both hands in front of her. "You know, Andy, you're still pushing me away." She left, pausing in the hallway to stare at him before heading toward the back door.

"Well, that was just great, Andy," he muttered. Danny was frowning at him. "Not you, too. Well, don't you worry. You're going to see your mommy and daddy real soon. But first, you're going to help your godfather find some papers in Caroline's desk. It's gonna be fun, okay?"

Andy carried Danny to the sunroom, where his mother's desk was. She had a day timer and papers there, and he planned to go through them and see if he could find anything on the grant mysteriously disappearing—and whether his mother had her hand anywhere in it.

CHAPTER
Twenty-Two

"Thanks, Andy, for bringing our baby home." Becky perched in a rocker in the corner of the small living room.

"Becky, let me take him. You have to be tired." Diana held out her arms and stepped around Andy and Brad. Neil was hovering in her fridge, and Jed was sitting on the loveseat with his father.

"Diana, I am tired, but never too tired to hold my grandson. Sit down and put your feet up, because I'm sure Danny's going to need you soon. Neil, while you're hovering in that kitchen, put on some coffee, because we have a lot to talk about."

"You know this house isn't big enough for everyone." Diana went to go sit on the sofa, but Jed patted his knee, and she found herself drawn to him. She slid onto his lap and leaned against his shoulder.

She was so tired, emotional, and weary that she took a moment to shut her eyes. It had been a long day, and she treasured the support she had from Jed's family.

"You're not going to fall asleep, are you?" Jed's large,

calloused hand rubbed her shoulder and down her bare arm.

"No, I'm just … well, today was a lot." Diana went to sit up, to slide off his lap, but Jed held her.

"You're comfortable here. Don't get up."

Brad's cowboy boots clicked on the floor. He shoved a hand in his pocket. "I think we all need to talk about what the doctor said."

Andy was leaning against the wall close to the door. "Why do I feel like I've been left in the dark? Maybe you could fill me in, someone?" He glanced at Diana briefly, then at Jed, Brad, Rodney, and Neil, who strode in with a chicken leg shoved in his mouth.

"Apparently our son here was hiding something the doctors found." Rodney glanced briefly at Jed as he spoke.

"Oh, come on, Dad," Brad said. "Andy, the doctors found a shadow that they say is a tumor. Where it is, it would be tricky to get out, and there is a lot of risk. But if he doesn't have it out, he'll be dead in a year." Brad paced in the small room and then sat on the arm of the sofa. "Isn't that about right, Jed? And the symptoms Jed's having now, the dizziness, slight loss of motor function, is only going to get worse. We need to expect seizures, stroke, blindness.… Did I forget anything?" Brad swung around and asked Neil.

Neil ripped off a piece of meat from the chicken leg, chewed, and said, "It's an aggressive tumor, and Jed is afraid of the consequences. Because it's a risky surgery, he could stroke out, be brain damaged, not be able to communicate and be a burden to his wife. Isn't that what you said, Jed?"

Jed just glared, and Diana smoothed over his shoulder and whispered to him, "Jed, don't be like that."

But Neil continued on. "And the worst case scenario is

he'll die on the table. But then, not having the surgery puts him in the grave." Neil tossed the half-eaten chicken leg on a plate on the table and wiped his hands together. "Except there is hope. Doctor Hardy is one of the top neurologists in the country. I made some calls, checked him out. He has a steady hand and calmness about him, too, and he's got some of the best imaging equipment available for a surgery like this. What he *didn't* tell you, Jed, is he's removed over a hundred tumors like this using the guided imagery." Diana noticed that Neil sounded so serious, and there wasn't even a hint of humor in the sparkle of his eyes. He actually looked more than a little pissed, and she hadn't seen that from him before.

"So, with this guided imagery and this amazing doctor, I don't understand why you're not going for it, Jed. You should be on the phone, lining it up right now." Andy was now standing beside Brad, shoulder to shoulder.

"Because there are risks, and it's not as easy as it sounds. The success rate isn't high. This guided imagery lets the doctor see exactly where to cut, but this being the brain, which is still very much a mystery, one tiny wrong cut and I'm no longer me," Jed muttered, and his arm slackened around Diana. "Neil, Brad, I want you two to take a minute and put yourself in my place, but really think of what the consequences would be if you were to have this surgery and wake up but not be able to talk, or maybe you couldn't move one side of you, maybe your thinking would be muddled and you would feel trapped inside a body that wouldn't cooperate and do what you wanted. Forget ever walking, riding a horse, and just being with your wife, because now she has to put a diaper on you because you can't even take a crap in the toilet, and she has to feed you like a baby, and then you're lying there for years and watching as she gets tired and weary and she has no one to hold her and tell her everything's going to be okay. And you watch as that bright, deep love that she's always shown you in her eyes changes and dims to something cold and bitter toward you."

Brad and Neil both shared a look of discomfort and then gazed at the ground, but it was Neil who pushed past Brad to the door and then paused, clearing his throat roughly. "I need some air." Then he opened the door and left, shutting it behind him.

Diana didn't move for a minute and then she slid around, watching the mirage of emotions on everyone: Becky as she rocked Danny, the solemnness of Andy and Brad and her father-in-law, Rodney. This was the first time Jed had shared his deepest fear. Before, she had known he was scared, but what she didn't know until this moment was how frightened he truly was of being a burden to her.

CHAPTER Twenty-Three

Jed turned off the hall light and followed Diana into their bedroom. His mom and dad had been the last to head out to one of the cabins. Neil and Brad were bunking in the other. Even when Andy left, he hadn't said a word, and he'd had the oddest expression on his face.

Jed didn't like the vulnerability he'd shown everyone. That wasn't him, and for a while he'd felt almost angry at Neil and Brad for cornering him into this position—but it wasn't their fault, he conceded, as he watched Diana with her back to him.

She went to lift off her t-shirt and then picked up a hairbrush from the top of the cluttered dresser, which was covered by her jewelry box, a pile of folded t-shirts they couldn't fit in the one small dresser, and a change jar where he tossed his pennies.

Diana started running the brush through her long red waves, and when it stuck on a knot, she started yanking on the brush to rip it through her hair.

Jed stepped over and grabbed her wrist. "Diana, don't."

She started trembling and then struggled to hold back the sob. Jed took the brush from her hand and set it on the dresser. He stepped back and sat on the bed, pulling Diana with him.

A thin stream of tears ran in a single line down her cheek. Her breath caught, but she managed to hold herself together as she sat on his lap.

"Diana…"

She leaned in and pressed her lips to his, placing both hands on his rough cheeks and just holding him, touching her nose to his.

"Jed, I love you so much. I need you to listen to me."

"Diana, please, honey. I'm tired." Jed really didn't want to talk about all of this anymore. He didn't like the vulnerability he was showing everyone, especially his wife. He was the strong one, the one who held them together.

"No, Jed." She tried to stand up, but Jed kept his hands firmly on her waist. "Jed, I understand what you're saying. My God, what you're talking about happening is an absolute nightmare and a worst-case scenario. But you need to understand something, how much I love you." She pressed her hand to her heart. "You are the first man who has ever gotten in here." She tapped her heart again. "You are my first breath in the morning, even when you make me so damn angry. You and me, we created Danny and this one." She picked up his hand and pressed it to her tummy. "To allow someone to cut into your brain is a terrifying thing. When you spoke from your heart tonight, I put myself in your place, and I can't say I wouldn't do the same. I would never want to be a burden to you or to Danny. I want you happy, and maybe I would try to be unselfish and want you to meet someone else after I was gone, to make you happy.

But that would be a lie. I'm not there, and I am selfish, because the thought of your hands never touching me again, and never tasting your kiss again—I can't go there yet, and neither should you. Because there is one thing I know about you, Jed. You're a fighter. Nothing gets you down. Hell, you come out swinging. This is the first time I've seen you allow anything to take you out. I've never known you for a quitter or to even give up without trying."

Jed watched her, wondering what she was up to. Her face was filled with passion but also a stubbornness and determination, like a guard dog at a gate. "Diana, you want me to take a chance at being a vegetable? I couldn't live like that."

"No, Jed, that's not what I'm saying. What I'd like is for you to take a chance to live, to take that chance and believe that you can beat this. My God, we've got a lot of things going for us. It's not game over, Jed. We have one of the best surgeons ready and willing. It's not like he hasn't done this before. You are a success at everything, I'm just asking you to try this with me. Don't go to that dark place and believe the worst. You would never let me do what you're trying to do to me. You asked your brothers to put themselves in your shoes, and I watched them as they did, and you scared the crap out of them, but I want you to do something for me."

"What do you want, honey?" He hesitated when he asked, because he could feel from the way she was guiding and asking that he wasn't going to like it.

"I want you to do the same for me."

He was confused, and it must have shown on his face, because as she next spoke, raised her eyebrows in a way he'd seen her do with a client.

"I want you to do exactly what you asked of Neil and Brad and put yourself in my place, as if it was me who faced the uncertainty. And I want you to feel and understand and take a couple days to do that."

Jed stared at his wife, wanting to refuse, but when he gazed into the pure blue of the eyes that had imprinted on his soul, he knew he couldn't refuse.

"All right." This time, he let Diana slip off his lap, undress, and slide under the covers, and when she patted the bed beside her, Jed joined her under the covers. As he held her, her breathing evened out. Jed realized it was going to be a long, sleepless night when the first image hit him of what his life would be like without Diana.

CHAPTER Twenty-Four

"Andy, you need to talk to me." Laura slid in bed beside Andy wearing a short white cotton nightgown. She leaned on her pillow and faced him.

He could feel her watching him, but he didn't want to talk. He'd walked away from her downstairs when she called out to him after he got home. He didn't even turn around, and he knew he should feel like an absolute dog for it, but he couldn't right now, because he had a giant hole in the center of where his heart should have been.

"Go to sleep, Laura." He tossed his forearm over his forehead and shut his eyes. He could feel her pull away again, and she turned on her side and gave him her back.

"You know, Andy, I care very much for Jed and Diana, and you not telling me what's going on has me thinking the worst for them. But the fact that you won't even talk to me, you dismiss me—I can't live like this. I can't allow Gabriel to go on seeing you treat me this way." She didn't look at him when she spoke, but even he could feel the dividing wall between them become thicker. Soon, neither would be able to reach the other, but he was so confused that he didn't know what he wanted anymore.

He was no one's hero. Hell, and Jed … he loved him and Diana. If Laura only knew where his thoughts had gone.

"Laura, I'm sorry. I know you care. It was just hard listening to Jed and my cousins tell me that Jed has some rare tumor that could kill him. The surgery that could save his life, he doesn't want to risk it, because it could leave him incapacitated."

Laura rolled over and then sat up, staring down at him with shock. He realized he should have tried to soften the blow.

"I'm sorry. I shouldn't have told you like that."

"My God, poor Diana. She must be beside herself. And Jed… and Danny… what a mess. I should go and see Diana. I'll call her in the morning." Laura rested her palm on Andy's shoulder and started to lean in to kiss him.

"Listen, Laura," he raised his hand and slid it over her shoulder to stop her, "don't call Diana. They have a lot on their plate right now. I'll talk to Diana myself tomorrow and see if there's anything I can do to help."

Laura pulled back and sat up. She stared at him and blinked, her face confused for a second before it filled with anger. "Are you in love with her?"

"What? No! Where would you ever come up with an idea like that?" Andy couldn't shake off this defensiveness, and then he felt his face flush.

"Oh, I see. Andy, we may be married on paper, and I was starting to wonder what it is that I've done wrong. I know I'm young, and then I started to wonder if you pity me, because I know you don't love me. But you have this wall you've erected around your heart. Don't get me wrong. You've gone above and beyond for Gabriel, getting him help, and I thank you for caring enough—"

"What the hell? Of course I care. Are you questioning my commitment to you?"

"No, Andy. I believe you're committed to me. You just don't love me, because you're in love with someone else. You may not want to admit it to yourself, but I was starting to wonder. With Diana, you've always had to race in as if you were going to take care of everything, which is so you. But it's different with her, and I finally realized it. You can't give me your heart, because you've already given it to her." Laura turned her back and slid her legs over the side of the bed.

Andy reached for her. "Where are you going?"

"I'm going to crawl in with Gabriel. I need some space, Andy." Laura reached for the terry cloth housecoat she'd draped over the easy chair by her side of the bed.

"This is ridiculous, Laura. I'm married to you. You're misreading my concern for my cousin and his wife."

"That's right, Andy, his wife. Your cousin's wife. It seems your concern should be directed more to Jed and not Diana, don't you think?" Laura didn't wait for Andy to answer; she left the bedroom, pulling the door closed softly behind her.

CHAPTER
Twenty-Five

Diana had left Jed alone for a week to think. She knew that what she'd asked of him was exactly what he was doing, searching his soul, all the while switching the roles and imagining it was she who was sick and she who had arbitrarily decided on no surgery. There was one thing she knew in the very center of her being about her husband: His level of commitment went above and beyond what she'd ever seen, and he lived and died by his word.

She knew she was taking a risk. When she told Jed's family that he needed time to think, they'd respected her wishes… but Brad said that though they would give him time to think, it couldn't take forever. They'd step in and sit down and have another heart to heart. Brad couldn't stay any longer, and the next morning, after speaking with Emily, his wife, he flew back to Hoquiam.

But he called every day and asked her if Jed had made a decision.

Neil was a different story. She really did love him, her brother-in-law, and enjoyed the time they had spent getting to know each other. But his lightheartedness and joking manner faded, replaced by a seriousness she hadn't known existed in him. He'd taken charge of their riding center, the construction, and threw himself into every part of it.

Diana was standing by the newly constructed round ring, leaning on the rail, just staring out into the mountains.

"Penny for your thoughts?"

She didn't hear Neil walk up to her as he leaned over the rail and just watched her with that goofy smile of his, which was damn charming. "Do you have a girlfriend?" she asked.

He laughed. "Do I have a girlfriend? Is that what you asked? Well, I'm not a monk by any means."

Diana reached over and patted his arm. "Oh, I know you're not a monk, but I just wondered. You've been here since Jed fell, but not once have I ever heard you mention a girl at home. Is there no one special in your life?"

"No one special, Diana. I mean, I date, but I'm not involved seriously with anyone." Neil looked almost wistful as he spoke.

"Well, that's a shame. I hope you meet the right girl, someone who can love you the way you deserve."

Neil chuckled again. "Well, I don't know if the ladies I date would agree with you. But thanks just the same, Diana. No, I am happy being single. You know, carefree life, go anywhere anytime, don't answer to anyone. I'm happy with that."

Diana watched Neil, and with the way he said it, she knew he was trying to convince himself of that very thing, but she also recognized loneliness in him. She knew by the way he watched her and Jed sometimes, when he didn't realize she was looking, that he too wanted something deep and meaningful.

Diana smiled at him, and her heart warmed. "You make me feel good, Neil. I'm so glad you're here with me and Jed. And just for the record, any woman who doesn't truly appreciate you can walk the other way."

Neil watched her thoughtfully and then gazed out at the mountains. "How's my little brother doing?"

"I gave him a lot to consider, to think about," Diana answered.

"You never told us what you said to him that's had him doing all this soul searching and pondering. Do you care to share it with your dashing and handsome brother-in-law?"

"Oh, Neil, I'm going to miss you when you go home." She stared at Neil, and he winked. "I just did what he did to you and Brad."

Neil blinked and glanced away, appearing somewhat confused. "You lost me."

"He told you and Brad to put yourself in his place. So I asked him to imagine it was me with this injury, and I decided to not risk this surgery, to not take a chance on life, and I asked him to imagine how he'd face his days with Danny alone, without me."

This time, Neil turned and faced her. "Wow, Diana. I always knew you were one smart lady, but that's not giving you enough credit. You're brilliant." This time, he smiled and patted the top rung of the corral, a little happier.

"You think it'll work?" Diana asked, because where Jed was concerned, she worried he'd still refuse the surgery.

"Oh, I know it'll work." Neil spoke with such conviction that Diana was puzzled.

"How do you know?"

"Because, Diana, in case you haven't noticed, my brother would walk into hell to go and get you and bring you back if that was where you went. And there's not a chance he'd ever sit back and allow you to make a decision like he did. He'd looked after you and nurse you himself, and he'd love you until the day you died, and it wouldn't matter a whit to him if you were the one lying in bed, staring at the ceiling, unable to talk, walk, or hold him. He wouldn't let you go."

As she watched her brother-in-law speak with such passion about Jed's love for her, she choked up, because although she knew Jed loved her deeply, she'd never allowed herself, until this moment, to really let it all sink in, how deep Jed's love was.

CHAPTER Twenty-Six

Neil seemed lost in thought as he smoothed his hand over the solid pine walls. He had always loved working with wood. Any minute he could, he leaned in and breathed the fresh wood smell. Jed watched his brother from the doorway, looking at the quality of workmanship Neil was known for. The tongue and groove placement of the wood strips set the ambiance for a charming western feel. This was more than he expected, than he had wanted, but, at the moment, it was also something of Neil he could treasure. Neil stared out through the solid glass of the viewing room to the covered arena of the riding ring. A dump truck was in the middle of the ring, dumping a load of sand, and a few men with rakes were spreading it around.

"Hey, I thought I'd find you in here," Jed finally interrupted.

Neil turned and blinked. "Didn't hear you come in."

"I noticed. Wow, I've got to say, I'm impressed with your work. Don't you miss it, working with your hands?"

Neil glanced at Jed and then ran his hands over the

paneling. His hands were usually clean—and, Jed suspected, manicured—but they were now covered in a mess of shavings and bits of white and dirt. Jed knew there were a few calluses, too.

"I enjoyed this. More than you know. Makes me really envy you and what you have here, that little something that's just yours," Neil said.

"You almost sound as if you regret working with Dad. I'm mean, what are you two doing with that huge cattle ranch you started? I thought you loved that new resort you were building, too."

Neil shrugged and then turned around, leaning against the wall and crossing his arms. "I did. I mean, I do. Don't get me wrong. I love putting together big deals, and that project for the resort is a challenge still, especially dealing with the Mexican government. But I don't know. I never imagined how fulfilling it would be to do something like you are. Something personal. On your own."

Jed looked around the glassed-in viewing room, which would seat the parents watching their special needs children on horseback. "Well, this was all you, brother dear. I wasn't putting out for something like this."

"Yeah, I guess I got a little carried away. Sorry about that."

Jed watched the boyish charm that always came so easily to Neil lift the melancholy mood he seemed to be in. "No, you're not, but I'm glad you did it, even though I was kind of choked in the beginning. In case I didn't say it, thank you."

"Jed, what do you want? Because to me it sounds like you're getting all weird about something, and I don't like the way this is sounding." Neil didn't move, but his unusually astute eyes took on a watchfulness, as if he suspected he was about to hear something he wasn't going to like.

"Listen, you should know I made a decision about the surgery." Jed strode to a bench pushed up against the wall and sat down.

Neil started toward him to help him. "Are you okay?"

"No, I'm fine. I just need to sit down."

Neil stepped in front of Jed. "The only answer I want to hear from you, Jed, is that you're having the surgery."

Jed could imagine Neil holding his breath, and he slowly shook his head. "It wasn't an easy decision to make, but my wife didn't play fair."

Neil chuckled. "I love Diana. You are so lucky she married you. She told me what she said, by the way. She has a lot of faith in you, and she loves you so much. So tell me, what part of what she said convinced you to have the surgery?"

"I promised her that I would spend time thinking about what I would want in her position, and I realized that if it was her, I'd find some way to strap her down and make her have the surgery. I'd never let her go without trying anything and everything. I wouldn't give her a choice. Neil, listen. I need to ask you a favor." Jed cleared his throat as all the dark worries that had plagued his mind throughout the past few days continued over and over.

"Anything, you know that." Neil swatted Jed's leg in a brotherly, loving way as he sat beside him on the bench.

"If something should happen to me, I want you to look after Diana, because as strong as she is, and she lets on to everyone that she can handle stuff, she's fragile inside her heart. She was hurt so badly as a kid that she's still vulnerable. I still see the hurt sometimes in her eyes. She took on some pretty bad stuff because of our uncle, even because of Andy. She has no family.... I don't want her alone again, ever. Things may be patched up now with Andy, but if I'm not here ... I just need you to get her out of here.

Take her and Danny with you and Mom and Dad. Don't let her come back here." Jed felt his throat tighten, and his eyes burned, so he coughed roughly.

Neil reached over and took his brother's hand. "I promise you I'll look after her. No matter what happens, I've got her back. So you go into that surgery with a clear mind and no worries. I won't let anything happen to her or Danny. She's part of our family, okay?"

Jed nodded and swallowed again. "Just one more thing."

Neil swung his arm across Jed's shoulder and squeezed gently. "You want me to make sure Andy stays away from her."

Jed gazed at his brother, surprised that he already knew. Then he nodded. "Yeah, far away."

CHAPTER Twenty-Seven

"Alright, Jed, you're looking great this morning, and I see your whole family is here again." Doctor Hardy strode into Jed's hospital room wearing blue scrubs.

Diana held Jed's hand so tightly that he lifted hers and kissed the back of it.

"Diana, it's okay."

She let out a shaky breath. "I know it is. I'm just… Doctor Hardy, please bring my husband back to me."

Doctor Hardy faced Diana on the other side of the bed, standing beside Rodney and Becky. "Jed is in good hands." There was something about him when he gave her all of his attention that instilled confidence. "Let's stay positive, everyone. Jed, are you ready to go up now? Everything's ready." Doctor Hardy accepted the chart from one of the nurses dressed in pink scrubs.

Jed cleared his throat. "Yup, let's get this show on the road."

"Okay, everyone. Jed, I'll see you up there." Doctor Hardy handed the chart back as a gurney was wheeled in by two orderlies and slid beside the bed. It was then that Doctor Gordon walked in and uttered something to Doctor Hardy, who nodded and said, "Okay, I'll take care of it."

"Is something wrong?" Diana was struggling to keep herself together now, and seeing that woman wasn't helping.

"Everything's fine, Diana. Doctor Gordon is just making sure everything's ready for the surgery." Doctor Hardy glanced at Doctor Gordon and inclined his head toward the door.

"Jed, we'll see you up there, and don't worry: You're in good hands with Doctor Hardy," Doctor Gordon said as she slipped out.

"Son, we'll be waiting here for you. Everything's going to be fine." Rodney slid his arm around Becky's shoulder, and Becky smiled through the glimmer of tears that brightened her eyes.

The gurney rail was slid down. "Okay, Jed, we need you to slide on over."

Diana leaned in and kissed Jed on the lips, tracing the veins that showed on his shaved head. She didn't want to let him go just yet. She wanted more time, and she felt the panic expand and rise up inside her, squeezing off all her air until she gasped and tears spilled down her cheeks.

"It's okay. We talked about this." He rested his hand on top of her head and kissed her back.

Diana gripped the faded blue hospital gown and twisted the fabric at his chest, burying her face into him.

She heard someone clear their throat, but she didn't care. She couldn't let him go, not yet.

"Hey… hey, Diana, come on. Look at me," Jed said.

But she couldn't, and she shook her head.

Jed wrapped his arms around her tight, and she heard him say, "Give us a minute."

Diana had no idea if everyone was still there or if they'd left as she struggled to catch her breath and control her sobs. Jed just rubbed her back and held her tight. He pressed his lips into her hair, against her forehead. She gazed up at him, and he tenderly kissed her lips, holding her face between his hands.

"I love you, Diana. I need you to be strong, okay? Weren't *you* the one who convinced me to have this surgery and trust Doctor Hardy, to have faith and believe that everything will be okay? That wasn't some other Diana, right?"

Diana used the sleeve of her blue shirt to wipe her eyes. "I know. I'm just not ready."

"I can call them back in if you want and tell them the surgery's off today. Is that what you want?"

"No… I'm just afraid. I can't lose you. Please promise me you'll come back to me." She gazed into those deep, loving eyes of the man who protected her, made her feel so safe.

"Diana, come on. I need you to be strong for me. You need to be there for Danny. We talked about this. Remember, we're taking this chance, and we're going to hope for the best because we can't settle for anything less. I'm coming back to you, I promise."

She held his determined gaze and took a shaky breath.

Jed glanced over her shoulder and said, "Neil, take her. Remember your promise."

"You go and you do this. We've got Diana. We'll take care of her." Neil slid his arms around Diana's shoulders. He pulled her back, and Jed slid over onto the gurney.

"Let's go," Jed said, and he wouldn't look back at Diana as he was wheeled out of the room past Brad,

Rodney, Becky, and Andy, who lingered in the hall with Laura.

Diana cried and felt her body sag, and her legs would have given out on her if Neil hadn't been behind her, holding her up.

CHAPTER Twenty-Eight

Jed was wheeled into the operating room, which was filled with high-tech equipment. Nurses and other OR staff were wearing gowns and gloved up. All had caps over their hair. Doctor Gordon wandered in just as Jed slid onto the table. An IV was inserted in his arm, and he was covered with a blue sheet.

"Jed, are you ready?" Doctor Gordon wore a mask as she leaned over him, but he'd recognize those beautiful dark eyes anywhere.

"Not really, but let's get this going."

She held the mask to her mouth and nodded.

Jed reached out to touch her arm. "Hey, do me a favor. Get me back to my wife in one piece, and if there's any chance it's not going to work, close me up. Make sure Doc Hardy closes me up."

Doctor Hardy strode in, hands in the air and on Jed's other side. "Jed, we're going to put you under now. We need you to start counting back from ten."

"Promise me," he said to Doctor Gordon, but everything dimmed before she could answer. He didn't see her hesitate as she glanced up at Doctor Hardy, and he didn't see her nod.

"How long have they been in there?" Diana hadn't sat for the past three hours. She'd paced the waiting room, the same circle in the checked carpet, at least a hundred times. She'd even taken to counting the squares as a way to keep from going crazy.

Neil leaned against the window, crossing his booted feet in front of him. Brad was trying to recline in one of the waiting room chairs, but they weren't made for solid six-foot cowboys made of nothing but lean muscle. Rodney and Becky were sitting across from Laura and Andy.

"It's only been an hour since you last asked. Maybe you should get out of here for a while, Diana. We could go out for dinner, take your mind off this," Andy suggested.

But Diana kept walking. "No, I'm not going anywhere. You guys go for dinner."

Andy pulled himself out of his chair, and Laura didn't say a word. "Diana, how about a walk just to clear your head?" He stood right in front of her, watching her, and she knew there was concern there.

"Andy, maybe you should take your wife out for dinner. Brad, Mom, Dad, maybe you'd like to go with them. I'll stay here with Diana." Neil was behind her and slid his arm around her shoulder.

Diana realized there was something going on between Andy and Neil. "Neil, you don't need to stay. Why don't you all go and take a break."

"I'm not hungry, but I'm going to call my wife," Brad

said. "Give her an update as to what's going on. She's damn worried and about ready to pack up all the kids and drive out here." Brad hefted himself from the chair and pulled up his jeans, and he slapped Andy between the shoulders. "Come on, cousin. Bring that pretty wife of yours. I'll walk you out."

Andy hesitated, but Laura stood up and slid her cloth purse over her shoulder. She walked around Brad and touched Diana's arm. "Can I bring you anything?"

Diana hugged Laura and felt her stiffen for a moment. "You go. Thanks for being here, though. Oh, could you do something for me? I don't want to leave, but I'm worried about Danny. Could you call Jules and check and see if Danny's okay?"

"Of course I will. I'll go find out for you. I'll go down now with Brad and call." She turned to leave and glanced up at Andy, but he made no move to go with her, so she stepped around him and walked out.

Brad studied Andy, shifting his gaze to Andy's departing wife and then back to him. "I hope you're going after her."

Andy hesitated a second, let out a heavy sigh, and then left after Laura.

Brad exchanged a worried glance with Neil.

"Is there something going on I should know about?" Diana asked, crossing her arms.

"No, just Andy's got to figure out a way to be a husband and look after his wife." Rodney spoke up and then patted Becky's knee. "How about some fresh air or a bite to eat?"

"No, I'm staying with Neil and my daughter-in-law, but you go," Becky said.

"Mom, Dad?" Brad asked.

"Go on, son. Tell Andy to take his wife out for dinner and that we'll let him know if we hear anything."

Brad hesitated and stared at the Friessen family vigil. He raised his cell phone in the air and said, "Let me update Emily, and then I'll be right back."

CHAPTER Twenty-Nine

Diana squeezed the cardboard cup with the dreg of bitter hospital coffee. She perched against the glass window, looking down on her family in the waiting room. Rodney and Becky were dozing, with her head in his lap. Brad sat with his arms crossed and his eyes closed. His chin rested against his chest as he softly snored.

Neil slid beside her, pressed his shoulder against hers and nudged. "You've held up really well, Diana. Why don't you get some sleep?"

She shook her head, feeling bone-weary and tired, with a heavy caffeine buzz from all the coffee she'd downed. She felt all shaky, but it was from the caffeine, which wasn't smart, considering the complicated circumstances.

She was sweaty and sticky too, and she realized she probably smelled. She was almost tempted to take a whiff of her underarm, but that would be too odd around Neil.

He must have sensed what she was thinking. "I'm sure we could all use a chance to clean up." He glanced at his thin gold watch. The white shirt he wore under the jean jacket, now tossed over one of the chairs, was rolled up to just below his elbows.

"How long has it been since the last update?"

"Two hours." Neil sighed, pressed his hands into her stiffened shoulders, and rubbed.

"What did that nurse say again?" Diana was struggling not to read more into the few words she had said.

"She said the surgery was going well, that Doctor Hardy expects a few more hours yet. I know it's not much to go on, Diana." Neil kept rubbing her shoulders. "You're doing fine. It shouldn't be much longer, and if I know my brother, he's going to pull though this. He's strong and he's determined. . . ."

The floor squeaked as Doctor Hardy hurried into the waiting area. Diana stepped forward, watching the older doctor in sweat-stained scrubs with the blue cap on his hair. He yanked it off, and Diana didn't miss how tired he looked, too.

"Mom, Dad, Brad," Neil called, and the chairs squeaked.

"Doctor Hardy, how is my husband?"

"Well, the surgery took longer than I expected. There was some unexpected bleeding—"

"What do you mean? Is my husband okay?" Diana couldn't keep the emotion from rising in her voice.

"Diana, let Doctor Hardy finish." Neil slid his arm around her shoulder. Brad stood beside her on her other side. Maybe they thought she was going keel over.

"Doctor Hardy, we need you in here now." Doctor Gordon hurried in, wearing the same blue scrubs, but her eyes were filled with worry.

"What's wrong? Is it Jed?" It was Rodney who asked, and it was the first time Diana heard his voice shake.

"I'll be back." Doctor Hardy didn't wait but turned

and ran just as the overhead speaker announced a code blue.

Becky covered her mouth and seemed to slump in Rodney's arms as a cry erupted from her. Diana didn't know what to do as she pulled away from Neil and sat in one of the chairs. Brad covered his mouth as if to cough, but she could tell he was fighting his emotions, and Neil watched her with misery in his sad brown eyes.

"What happened?" Andy strode in, dressed as he always was in a dark shirt and blue jeans. Diana barely registered Laura behind him, wearing a light sweater.

Neil roughly cleared his throat, shaking his head as he turned away. His shoulders shook, and Brad rested a hand on Neil's shoulder.

It was Brad who said, "Something happened. Doctor Hardy just raced out of here. We don't know if it was Jed—"

"I think my husband just died," Diana said, and then she glanced at Laura. "I'm going to get my son."

Diana, for the first time during this emotional roller coaster, felt a wave of calm she couldn't explain.

Becky was sobbing softly, and Rodney stared at her with red eyes glossed over with tears. Neil was running his hands through his hair roughly.

"Diana, wait. We don't know anything yet." Brad was right there, but his voice was thick with emotion.

"I can take you, Diana. I'll drive you back to the estate." Andy held out his hand to Diana, but it was the look in Brad and Neil's eyes that had her staying where she was, not taking his hand. When she glanced at Laura standing behind Andy, she could see her stunned look as if the girl had been slapped. Diana said nothing, but she studied everybody and watched as Laura turned and left.

CHAPTER *Thirty*

"Go after your wife, Andy." It was Diana who calmly sat and watched as Laura walked. It was a moment that reminded her so much of what she'd lived before, in another life, but she was watching it happen to someone else.

Neil turned around, and tears stained his cheeks. He stepped around Brad and took the chair beside Diana, and he didn't hesitate to slide his arm around her shoulder to pull her close, to kiss her forehead. "We're going to wait, okay? Then I will take you to Danny and we'll pick him up." Diana didn't need to look at Brad, Neil, Rodney, and Becky, because she felt their love so deeply for Jed, but it was the first time she realized it was for her, too.

"Okay, folks." There was a rustling behind Andy. Doctor Hardy burst in with Doctor Gordon.

"Was that my husband who coded?" Diana asked as everyone else waited.

"Yes, there were some complications."

Becky let out a deep, wretched sob.

"We brought him back, and he's in ICU."

"Thank God," Brad said.

Heavy sighs and tears were on everyone's face when Diana looked at her family.

Neil squeezed Diana's shoulder, but he continued to hug her. "What happened, Doctor Hardy?"

"During surgery, there was unexpected bleeding. I got it under control, but the biggest concern now is infection and swelling. The next twenty-four hours are critical. Jed apparently suffered a seizure, and he coded. We brought him back, and he's stable now. We've medicated him, but we need to watch him closely." Doctor Hardy took in everyone surrounding him and then focused on Diana. "I know you want to see your husband, that you all want to see Jed, but I can't let you all in just yet. Diana, I can give you a few minutes. Everyone else, you'll need to wait."

Diana stood up with ease, but Neil helped her. "Doctor Hardy, how did the surgery go?" she asked. "Did you get out the tumor, all of it? Is there any damage, anything else that we need to know about Jed, any complications?"

"Diana, we're not going to know much until Jed wakes up. Sometimes, there can be some lapse in motor skills, but full function can return in time. I did get all of the tumor. Okay, so let's just take it in steps now: the next twenty-four hours and when Jed wakes up." Doctor Hardy shook Rodney's hand and held tight. "Diana, Doctor Gordon here will show you in to Jed."

Diana had almost forgotten the other woman was there.

"Well, let's get you to your husband," Doctor Gordon said.

Thank God for Neil was all Diana could think as he walked her with Doctor Gordon down to the ICU, to the glassed-in room where Jed was.

Neil left her at the door, and when she glanced back,

he watched her and his brother. Jed was hooked up to just about everything, tubes and wires sticking out of him. His head was wrapped in a thick white bandage, but he didn't have a tube down his throat this time, and he was breathing on his own.

"You can hold his hand. Just don't touch his head. I'll get you a stool so you can sit beside him."

The tall doctor wheeled a high stool over and Diana sat, sliding her hand under Jed's. She bent down and kissed the back of his hand. "Jed, you scared the life out of me. Please don't go. I need you to fight like you promised you would. Come back to me and Danny. Your family's here. Your brothers, you know, have been taking care of me, and for the first time, Jed, I know I'm not alone without you."

Doctor Gordon watched her from the other side of the bed. She checked an IV tubing and smiled shyly. "It will help Jed if you keep talking to him."

"Doctor Gordon, you're in love with my husband, aren't you?"

The woman's eyes widened, and the nurse who was behind her coughed and then slipped out of the room.

"I saw the way you looked at him when I walked in the first time and saw you together, the way you touched him. Even in my home, when you tried to dismiss me..." Diana wasn't ordinarily so blunt, but she was exhausted, physically and emotionally spent.

"Your husband loves you so deeply and so much, and I'm sorry for what you walked in on. It wasn't my intention…" She gritted her teeth and rested her hands on the metal side rail of the bed, glancing away as if gathering her thoughts. "I envy you, having someone like your husband watching over you, loving you the way he does. You're his first concern, you and your son and what should happen to him. He loves you so much he's afraid to burden you, and I envy that. So yes, I care deeply for your husband because he loves *you* so deeply. Please don't be jealous of me, and I am sorry for what you walked in on. I care for him. At your home that day, Jed didn't want you to know about the tumor and how grave the situation was. I was bound by doctor confidentiality, and I admit I could have handled it better. I was just annoyed at Jed and frustrated because he wouldn't tell you. I was trying to talk sense into him. I was just glad that your brother-in-law Brad insisted on staying and made your brother tell him. It made my job easier. I was tempted to break confidentiality and come and talk to you." She tapped the rail. "Stay as long as you want. I'll see that the nurses let you stay."

Diana watched her walk away as the glass door slid open. "Doctor Gordon?"

The doctor paused and glanced back at Diana. "Yes?"

"Thank you."

Doctor Gordon smiled, inclined her head, and left, pausing outside to speak with Neil.

Diana turned back to Jed. She placed her hand over his and bent down to kiss it. "Jed, I'm here. And I'm not going anywhere until you wake up."

CHAPTER
Thirty-One

"Laura, wait. Where do you think you're going?" Andy jogged after Laura outside the Seattle hospital, where she hurried away.

She didn't stop until he caught up with her and grabbed her arm, pulling her around. "Laura, what is wrong with you?" Andy snapped.

"Wrong with me? Are you kidding me? Andy, I may be your wife in name, but that's not how you see me or treat me. What the hell was that in there?" she snapped.

"What are you talking about?" Andy wasn't about to elaborate. He was feeling overwhelmed and selfish, and it irritated him to have to chase Laura down. "You know what? You should have stayed home. That's my cousin in there who may have just died, and here you are, pulling some prima donna act."

Laura glared at the hand that held her arm, and then she pulled her arm away. "Andy, I've known for a while you've had feelings for your cousin's wife. I saw how you were with Diana after Jed's accident. Even before. I just didn't admit it to myself. You're in love with her, and don't think I don't realize you wish I'd just go away, because with me gone and your cousin gone, maybe you'll be free to go after Diana. Well, go after her, because you're free."

"Don't do something you're going to regret, Laura. If it wasn't for me, Gabriel wouldn't have the help he has now, and you wouldn't have all those nice things, clothes, jewelry, everything I've bought you, and you'd be living in some slum with some sleazebag trying to take advantage of you."

Laura stumbled as if she'd been slapped. Her face paled, and tears glossed over her eyes. "You're right, Andy...."

"Andy," Brad shouted from behind him, "Jed's okay." He jogged up in cowboy boots. "He's in ICU. They said he's stable."

Laura touched his arm. "Andy, you better go on up and be with your family."

Brad looked away and slapped Andy on the shoulder. "I'll see you up there. Just thought you'd want to know."

"Thanks, Brad. I'll be right up." Andy watched Brad hurry back to the front doors of the hospital. When he turned back to Laura, she was watching Brad walk away.

"Listen, Laura, I'm sorry. I shouldn't have said that.... I didn't mean it to sound like that." And he did feel bad. He didn't want to hurt her. Not like this.

"Go back inside. Sometimes we say things in anger that we later regret, but only because it hurt the other person." She patted his hand again. "I truly believe you love your cousin Jed, and it must be difficult for you to love both Diana and Jed."

"Laura, let's go inside." Andy didn't hold her hand this time, as she crossed her arms and stepped back.

She shook her head. "You go." She stepped back again.

"Well, don't stay out here too long." Andy glanced back

at the doors. "I'll see you up there." He strode back toward the front doors and glanced back to see Laura still standing there, watching him. He felt horrible for what he had said and hoped she wouldn't stay down there too long and sulk. Surely she must realize he cared for her. Love was a deep, powerful emotion filled with pain and hurt, something that connected him and Diana. But Laura, she didn't know what he felt for her aside from the fact that she was his wife. Maybe it was time they took that honeymoon he never booked and really got to know each other. He owed her that, and he would try after Jed was out of the woods and back home, he told himself, because he wasn't his father. He wouldn't be his father, and Laura wasn't his mother.

Brad had just stepped onto the elevator.

"Brad, wait up."

Brad reached out and held the door. "Isn't your wife coming?"

"No, she just needs some air. She'll be up soon," Andy said as the elevator doors slid closed.

CHAPTER *Thirty-Two*

"He's awake. He's hungry, too." Diana burst into tears of joy and laughed before she choked on a sob.

Neil was right in front of her in that waiting room, and he pulled her into a tight hug, and then Brad, Rodney, and Becky joined. She was surrounded by arms. She swiped at her cheeks.

"When do we get to see him?" It was Brad who asked.

"I don't know. The doctor's in with him now and asked me to step out. They're examining him."

"Well, how did he sound?" Brad squeezed her shoulders as she stepped back and took in the faces of her family: Becky, Rodney, Neil, and Andy, who was alone behind them.

"He sounded pissed. Said his head hurt. He asked if I would make him a pie."

"Oh, way to go, Jed. First thing to ask when you wake up is for your wife to make you a pie," Neil blurted, grinning with a devilish spark back in his eyes.

"Neil, I will gladly make him the biggest, juiciest pie ever. Whatever he wants."

"Okay, good news," Doctor Hardy said in a way that lightened Diana's heart. "He's responsive, and I can't see anything that's led me to believe he won't have a full recovery."

"Can we see him?" Becky asked.

"One at a time. But don't let him overdo it." Doctor Hardy gazed at all of them, his light eyes suddenly filled with joy. "Ah, what the hell. You all go on in and see him."

THEY ALL FOLLOWED THE DOCTOR, but it was Brad who glanced back at Andy. "Are you coming?"

Andy's cell phone rang, and he reached in his pocket and pulled it out. "You go ahead. Looks like I forgot to turn this off."

Brad left him, and Andy darted into the back of the waiting room so the hospital staff didn't see him. "Hi."

"Andy, it's Jules. You need to come home."

"What's wrong? Is it Danny?" Andy asked.

"It's your wife, Andy. Danny's fine. I think Laura is leaving."

Andy disconnected the phone and slipped it into his back pocket. He wiped his face, furious at Laura for pulling this now. He strode out of the waiting room and down to Jed's room, watching through the glass as everyone surrounded the bed. Jed's face lit up with a bright smile, and laughter echoed into the hall. Andy also realized there was no place for him in there, so he went to the elevator, stepped inside, and the doors closed.

CHAPTER Thirty-Three

"Laura," Andy shouted out as he strode in the front door, letting it swing shut behind him. He took the stairs two at a time and was halfway up when Jules called out, "Andy, she's gone."

Jules was staring up at him in a dark brown house dress and white apron. Her large, round face appeared distressed in a way Andy had not seen before. She wasn't even wringing her hands, and that was something she did often when something upset her.

Andy's stomach flipped, and he hesitated only a second before racing up the stairs to their bedroom at the end of the long hall. He pushed open the door and took in the neatly made four poster bed, the easy chair, and the loveseat in front of the fireplace. There was no mess, nothing out of place. Andy yanked open Laura's drawers, where her clothes were supposed to be, and everything he'd bought for her, all the clothes, were still there. He yanked open the door to the walk-in closet, and the outfits and dresses he'd insisted she buy were still there. He wondered, as he glanced at the shoes, if she'd worn any of it. Even the necklaces and diamond earrings in the open jewelry case on the dresser appeared untouched.

Jules was standing inside the doorway now, her big arms crossed.

"Where is she, Jules?" he barked as he stormed into the bathroom and rummaged the medicine cabinet, the shower, but nothing was missing. He turned around and almost stepped on Jules, who was now right behind him.

"She didn't take anything, Andy, except a small backpack with a few of Gabriel's clothes and that worn duffle bag of hers with some of her old clothes she wouldn't part with. I'm pretty sure she took nothing from what you bought her. I'm sorry, Andy. I don't know where she went or what happened. I've never seen her look the way she did when she walked in here, lost, distressed. What happened, Andy?"

Andy shut his eyes when the reality of what he'd done sunk in. He was such a bastard. She didn't deserve to be treated the way she was. He sat on the side of the large jetted bathtub and then leaned down, dropping his face in his hands. He just shook his head.

"I tried to talk to her, to get her to stay. She'd been crying. Her eyes were red and swollen. She came home in a cab, Andy. She didn't have enough money to pay the cab driver. I took care of it for her. She felt horrible and said she'd pay me back. Andy, I don't understand why your wife has not a cent on her."

"Because I'm a bastard who's controlled everything, Jules. She had no reason to have money. I paid for everything."

"Andy, why?"

Jules gave him a look filled with such disappointment that he was filled with anger. He didn't want to be judged by her, so he brushed her off. "Where is she, Jules? She has no money, so she can't get far. She doesn't have a car. I drove her everywhere."

"No, you controlled her right good, didn't you? Aida said she'd drive her wherever she wanted to go. Aida hasn't come back either, Andy, so I don't know where she is."

Andy towered over Jules, and she flushed and looked down. His jaw slackened only because he was gritting his teeth so hard his jaw ached, but in that moment he also felt embarrassed for how he had treated Laura. He remembered the look she'd given him outside the hospital when he'd thrown in her face how it was he who had pulled her from the gutter and bought all this stuff for her and for her son. She hadn't said a word, and he could see now what he hadn't noticed before. None of it meant anything to her.

"Where does Aida live?" Andy demanded.

"She's in town. Her address and phone number are in the office. All the staff information is." Danny cried out from down the hall. "I better go check on the baby." Jules started down toward him.

"No, I'll get him." Andy headed down toward the nursery, where his godson slept. He lifted Danny, who was sitting up in the large white crib he'd ordered the first day Danny stayed over. "Hey, you, it's okay. I won't let anything happen to you. Nothing at all." He kissed Danny's head and then strode to the window. He gazed out onto the massive front lawn, at the staff who worked for him, and the reality hit home of how alone he now was.

CHAPTER Thirty-Four

"He's here." Diana slid out of the backseat of the new truck Neil had bought for Jed. Diana opened the passenger door, and Jed took her hand before stepping out, his light hair already growing in, hiding the scar from the incision.

Becky carried a gurgling, noisy Danny, who patted his hands together and called out, "Da da." He bounced, reaching wide eyed for Jed.

Jed reached for Danny and hugged him. "Oh, I missed you, little boy." Then he pulled Diana beside him and into his arms with Danny. Jed kissed the top of her head, loving the way she'd left her deep red hair long and loose for him.

Streamers were draped across the front of the house with a sign that said *Welcome home, Jed.*

Rodney reached across and ran his hand over the short, bristled hair growing in. "Looks good on you, son. How about that? Your wife doesn't have to nag you anymore to get a haircut."

"Yeah, well, I may keep it this short. Will definitely use less shampoo, that's for sure." Jed laughed.

Diana poked him in the ribs. "Jed."

Jed pulled her tighter, with his baby boy in his other arm. "Mom, thanks for all this. Diana said you were planning a big surprise." Jed leaned down and kissed his mom without letting go of Danny or Diana.

Becky patted his cheeks. "I am so glad you're home. And how are you feeling, really, Jed?"

"I'm good, Mom, *really*. Doctor Hardy said I need to take it easy for the next little bit—"

"And he needs to see Jed again in a couple weeks and then again in six months," Diana interrupted, "but he was thrilled by Jed's progress. He said he hoped for really good and would have even been okay with just good, but he said this is the first time he's seen outstanding. That was exactly what he said about Jed, 'Expect good as new.' " Diana beamed up at him.

A truck horn honked as it pulled in and parked. Brad climbed out, along with his family: his wife, Emily, Trevor, Katy, and their little Becky, who was in her terrible twos.

Brad strode over and hugged Jed, patting his back and then kissing Diana. "Ah, you look good."

"Jed, good to see you, and I'm so glad you're doing better." Emily passed little Becky to her daddy so she could hug Diana. "I am so happy for you. I was so worried every time Brad called that I wanted to climb in the truck and drive out here." Emily patted Jed's arm. "Don't scare your wife like that again. You Friessen men are a handful."

Diana leaned in and hugged Jed again. "Yeah, you sure are, and I wouldn't miss one moment of it. Except maybe a little less drama, please."

Neil, Jed, and Brad chuckled.

"Well, let's get this party started." Jed started toward the barn. "But first I want a tour of our new riding center—and all the bells and whistles I know you added, Neil."

They all started toward the covered riding area, but Neil stopped when he glimpsed Andy standing off to the side. He didn't know he'd come, but it was the look on his cousin's face that had Neil saying, "I'll see you guys over there in a minute."

"Andy," he said as he clasped his cousin's hand and shook it, patting his shoulder. "Glad you could come."

"It's good to see Jed home. And he's doing well," Andy said, but he appeared so distracted, with a sadness Neil hadn't seen before.

"Laura didn't come with you?" Neil asked, and he watched Andy glance away. His jaw hardened as if he were chewing on something.

"She left me." When he looked back at Neil, his eyes had a faraway look filled with hurt.

"Oh, Andy, I'm sorry. Is it something you can work out?" Neil really didn't know what to say. He'd seen the way Andy watched Diana, and he imagined Laura must have figured it out, too.

"I don't know where she is. I don't know what can be saved or worked out." He wiped both hands over his face. "Sorry, Neil. I'm just worried because she has no money, and she took nothing."

Neil opened his mouth to say something sharp to reprimand him, but when he watched Andy now, he couldn't. "What are you going to do?"

"I don't know. But if you'll make my excuses, I'm going to slip out."

"Andy," Neil called out as his cousin started to leave. Andy stopped, but he didn't turn around. "It's none of my business, Andy, but in case no one has told you, you're not your parents. Laura is a nice lady. I hope you can find her."

Andy's back stiffened, and he glanced back at Neil with

an expression of remorse that Neil had never seen in his cousin before.

"I'm going to try."

Turn the page for a sneak peek of
RUNAWAY the next book in THE OUTSIDER SERIES
Available in print, eBook and audio

Andy is looking for his runaway bride. And when he finds her, he's in for a big surprise.

> ***"Just when you think the story can't get any hotter, you're sadly mistaken."***
>
> *— "Another hot Friessen Man. It is a pleasure watching Andy learn how to be a real husband and father." -Reviewer, Miranda*
>
> *—"This definitely proves money doesn't buy love. What a suspenseful love story." -Reviewer, April*

Six months ago, Laura walked out on the only man she's ever truly loved. Even though wealthy Andy Friessen has been looking for her what he doesn't know is the secret Laura has been hiding. And when Andy finds out he'll risk everything to get her back.

Chapter 1

"Are you Andy Friessen?"

Andy didn't bother to glance up from where he was bent over the hoof, picking mud and gravel from his three-year-old buckskin, Ladystar. Andy dug out the last dried chunk of mud, wanting to snap at whoever was bothering him. "Damn kid I hired didn't clean out her hoof after riding her," he muttered. He put her hoof down, and she stomped and pranced as Andy pressed his hand to her hind quarter. He wiped the sweat from his forehead and picked up her front hoof, starting to dig around the frog, picking out all the dried mud. Bent over as he was, Andy could see a pair of blue jeans on some man who was standing behind his horse. "I wouldn't stand there if I were you," he said, setting down the mare's hoof and standing up. "It's a good way to get yourself kicked."

A short man wearing shades and a tan sports coat stepped sideways around a pile of fresh manure. "I'm looking for Andy Friessen," the man said.

"Yeah, well, you found him. What do you want?" he

snapped, irritated because all he wanted to do was saddle the horse, head onto the trail, and ride for the next few hours without one more person asking him another stupid question. He just wanted some peace.

"You've been served." The man slapped court papers in his hand and then hurried the other way as if Andy was going to chase him down and pound the crap out of him.

"Hey, what the hell is this?" Andy barked at the man now jogging up the driveway.

Andy swore as he flipped open the document and read ***Petition for Divorce*** in bold black letters. Laura was suing him for divorce! He couldn't believe it. Hell, any woman would give her right arm to be married to him, to have his name. As he read on, he felt like ice shards were ripping through his veins as he saw Diana Friessen's name written at the bottom as the lawyer of record. She was his cousin Jed's wife and the one woman he'd probably go to his grave loving. How could she do this to him and not call him? Did Jed know?

He hadn't heard from Laura in over six months. She'd walked out the door without saying goodbye to him, taking her son, Gabriel, with her and leaving everything he'd bought for them behind. Andy had been furious at first. Hell, he'd even tracked her down to where she'd been staying with the old cook, Aida, who still worked for Andy and his family. But Laura had refused to speak with him, and Aida sent him away and asked him not to come back again. Six months ago, he had expected Laura to return home to the estate with her tail tucked between her legs. After all, she had no money, no family, and no resources, with a little boy to feed, clothe, and shelter. She needed him.

But she didn't come back. And she didn't phone.

Then he worried. He'd married her to protect her

when she'd been forced to live in her car after she couldn't pay rent because his mother had fired her when she worked as a maid—all because she'd knocked over a Christmas tree. When the sheriff had found her living in her car, the authorities took Gabriel and stuck him into a foster home that wasn't even fit to care for a dog. Andy had stepped in and married her to help her get Gabriel back. Why had he done it? Because the whole messed-up situation that had spiraled from bad to worse had been his fault.

As Andy read through the black print and legalese, he fought back a rising tide of anger and disbelief. Well, to hell with her. She appreciated nothing he'd done for her. What should he expect from someone so young and ungrateful and...? He stopped cold when an icy chill raced through him as he realized she'd asked for nothing from the divorce, not one red cent from him.

Andy came from one of the wealthiest families in the county; she could easily have asked for a fortune and gotten it even though they'd been married less than a year. Andy knew she wasn't a fool, and deep down he knew she was no gold digger. She was hurt and vulnerable and innocent, and he hadn't treated her with a lick of respect. The fact was that he was having a hard time admitting what a prick he'd been. He was ashamed of the way he'd taken charge of her life, of Gabriel's, without sharing anything of his life with her.

Well, to hell with her. He would just wash his hands of her and say good riddance. He crumpled the papers and went to stuff them in his pocket, then stopped when he glimpsed the back door open. Aida, the old cook, stepped out of the staff entrance of the vast Friessen mansion, carrying her coat and purse, having finished her work for the day.

Andy rested his arm against Ladystar's side. The mare

nickered and then stomped her hoof impatiently, but Andy patted her flank. "Just give me a minute, girl."

He stepped away. His feet obviously had a mind of their own, because the last thing he should have been doing was exactly what he was doing, making a beeline straight to Aida, cutting her off before she reached her old compact car.

"Aida, please tell me where she is. I know she moved out of your place," Andy called. He strode toward Aida, really digging in to each step, swatting the papers in the air as if taking out a few flies here and there.

For a short woman in her seventies, Aida was quick as she darted around him. Andy spun around and jogged after her. This wasn't the average stroll he took when walking with a woman.

Aida yanked the hairnet off her short, graying bob, reaching behind her back to pull on her apron strings. "Andy Friessen, don't keep asking me, because I won't tell you." She jerked open the driver's door and tossed her apron and purse in. Andy gripped the top of the door so she couldn't slam it closed in his face again, as she'd done yesterday, last week, and every time he'd tried to talk to her after work. In the kitchen, she would ignore him and then order him out. When he didn't comply, she would threaten to quit.

Andy couldn't blame Laura for leaving him, really. After all, they never had a chance to get to know each other. There was no burning love between them, the kind where he would count the minutes—the seconds until he could see his wife again; the kind that would distract him and drive him crazy, his whole being sizzling in anticipation of that one touch, that smile, or just hearing her voice, the kind of deep love that would touch him inside his soul so that the thought of never seeing or hearing her again would shred his every last bit of good sense and he would question his will to live without her. No, there was none of that with Laura. He did, however, feel responsible for her even now, with these cursed papers burning a hole in his hand. Just what the hell was the matter with him?

Maybe it was because she was so young. She'd just turned twenty-one last week, and even though he hadn't seen her or heard from her, he had found himself buying her a gift—a solid gold locket. Of course, it remained wrapped upstairs in their room along with all of the other things he'd bought her. He had bought the gift on a whim, as he hadn't seen Laura or spoken to her since that day outside of the Seattle Hospital where Jed was recovering from surgery, when Andy had been a total ass. In hindsight, he'd love to go back and kick himself in the butt, to apologize, to not walk away and leave her standing there alone. She was honest, hardworking, and her only sin had been getting pregnant at fifteen with Gabriel and being cast into the street by her judgmental parents, who were too worried about how the situation would look and how it would influence Laura's younger brothers. Andy had never met her parents, and didn't plan on it, but he still couldn't soften his heart toward them.

He swung the paper in the air again. "She filed for divorce. I was just served. I need to talk to her, Aida."

The old woman stared straight ahead and said nothing.

"She asked for nothing, Aida. How is she paying rent? Where is she getting money from? Does she have a job? What about Gabriel?"

"Andy, let go of my door." Aida stared up at him with her plump, wrinkled face and her gray eyes, which were etched with tiny red lines as if they'd seen every good and bad thing in life.

Andy yanked out his wallet. "I need you to give her

some money. How is she going to look after herself?" He pulled out all of the bills, knowing there were only a thousand dollars there. He handed the stack to Aida, and she stared at the bills as if they were dirty. "Aida, did you give her the money I sent before? I know she didn't cash the check I gave you," Andy said, pleading.

She pursed her pale, wrinkled lips. She didn't look away, though she did appear to be considering what to say to Andy. Andy had no doubt she'd go to her grave without parting with one secret of where Laura was hiding.

"I gave her the cash, but do not ask again where the girl is, as I won't tell you. I promised her, Andy. She doesn't want to see you again," Aida said. However, bless her heart, she did fold the cash and tuck it into a side pocket of her purse before folding her plump body into the compact car.

"Aida, I want to see her and Gabriel. Could you ask her to meet me. Please?" Andy squatted down so that he didn't have to look down on the old cook.

"Andy, she has a right to be angry with you. You treated her horribly and made her feel as if she was a nuisance to have around. You may have married her to protect her and Gabriel, but the way you talked to her after you were married, it was as if she still worked for you. And she was a nice bed warmer, too, hey?"

Andy blushed, which was something he didn't do. Aida was right. He'd bedded her, but he hadn't shared one aspect of his life with her. Time did have a way of opening his eyes, especially when she'd taken nothing. He was worried about how she was managing to pay for anything just to survive, let alone feed her and Gabriel.

"Aida, I am a bastard, I admit, but I'm worried about her. Telling her I'm sorry doesn't even begin to make up for what I've done. I know words mean nothing, but please just ask her to meet me. How am I supposed to make things right if she won't see me?"

Aida gripped the steering wheel. She let out a heavy sigh. "Andy Friessen, I will talk to Laura, but I won't make you any promises."

Andy reached in and patted her arm because he sensed he was getting through to the tough old bird. If he could convince Aida he was sincere and win her over, she would be his best ally and his best hope to reach Laura. "I'll see you tomorrow, Aida, and thank you. Please tell her I'll go wherever she wants to meet, at any time, please..." Aida shut her door and Andy stood behind one of the ranch hand's pickups, watching as Aida drove away down the long, paved driveway, beside the manicured lawns and gardens, out to the highway.

His cell phone rang, and he yanked it from his back pocket. "Andy Friessen," he answered, distractedly watching the now empty driveway.

"Hey, Andy. This is Brian. I've got some news on that wife of yours," answered a familiar voice. Brian Rivers was a private detective that Andy had hired a few months back to keep an eye on Laura.

"If it has anything to do with her filing for divorce, I already know. I was just served by some law school dropout."

There was a clatter and brief silence on the other end. "No. I didn't know that. Well, how about that? So how much is she trying to bleed you for?"

"Not a damn thing, so I want to know where she's getting her money from. Is she still in that old house at the edge of town?" Andy watched Ladystar, who was tied to the rail outside the barn. The feisty thing was getting impatient, stomping her front hoof and pawing at the ground.

"Well, that's why I'm calling. She moved. Your cousin

and that pretty redheaded wife of his were there, and they picked her up. She doesn't have a car. She's staying out at their place. They built a studio above their barn and I'm pretty sure they moved her in."

Andy remembered Jed telling him just last week about the new studio. Hell, he'd even seen it; a cozy open loft with a kitchen, bathroom, living room, and bedroom all in one area. He thought Jed had told him it was for a manager he was hiring.

Then he wondered... No, it couldn't be. Laura was the manager and working for his cousin? Jed wouldn't do that to him and not say anything. But then, as the reality sank in and the stiff white paper burned a hole in his hand, Andy remembered that Diana, Jed's wife, had filed this petition, and not one of them had said squat. "I gotta go," he said.

"But, wait, don't you want to know—" Brian tried to interrupt.

"Not now, Brian. I've got to go. I have a cousin to visit."

About the Author

> "Lorhainne Eckhart is one of my go to authors when I want a guaranteed good book. So many twists and turns, but also so much love and such a strong sense of family."
>
> (LORA W., REVIEWER)

New York Times & USA Today bestseller Lorhainne Eckhart is best known for writing Raw Relatable Real Romance where "Morals and family are running themes." As one fan calls her, she is the "Queen of the family saga." (aherman) writing "the ups and downs of what goes on within a family but also with some suspense, angst and of course a bit of romance thrown in for good measure."

Follow Lorhainne on Bookbub to receive alerts on New Releases and Sales and join her mailing list at Lorhainne-Eckhart.com for her Monday Blog, all book news, give-aways and FREE reads. With over 120 books, audiobooks, and multiple series published and available at all, retailers now translated into six languages. She is a multiple recipient of the Readers' Favorite Award for Suspense and Romance, and lives in the Pacific Northwest on an island, is the mother of three, her oldest has autism and she is an advocate for never giving up on your dreams.

> "Lorhainne Eckhart has this uncanny way of just hitting the spot every time with her books."
>
> (CAROLINE L., REVIEWER)

The O'Connells: *The O'Connells of Livingston, Montana are not your typical family. A riveting collection of stories surrounding the ups and downs of what goes on within a family but also with some suspense, angst and of course a bit of romance thrown in for good measure. "I thought I loved the Friessens, but I absolutely adore the O'Connell's. Each and every book has different genres of stories, but the one thing in common is how she is able to wrap it around the family, which is the heart of each story." (C. Logue)*

The Friessens: *An emotional big family romance series, the Friessen family siblings find their relationships tested, lay their hearts on the line, and discover lasting love! "Lorhainne Eckhart is one of my go to authors when I want* *a guaranteed good book. So many twists and turns, but also so much love and such a strong sense of family." (Lora W., Reviewer)*

The Parker Sisters: *The Parker Sisters are a close-knit family, and like any other family they have their ups and downs. Eckhart has crafted another intense family drama… "The character development is outstanding, and the emotional investment is high…" (Aherman, Reviewer)*

The McCabe Brothers: *Join the five McCabe siblings on their journeys to the dark and dangerous side of love! An intense, exhilarating collection of romantic thrillers you won't want to miss. — "Eckhart has a new series that is definitely worth the read. The queen of the family saga started this series with a spin-off of her wildly successful Friessen series." From a Readers' Favorite award—winning author and "queen of the family saga" (Aherman)*

Lorhainne loves to hear from her readers! You can connect with me at:

www.LorhainneEckhart.com

lorhainneeckhart.le@gmail.com

Also by Lorhainne Eckhart

The Outsider Series

The Forgotten Child (Brad and Emily)
A Baby and a Wedding *(An Outsider Series Short)*
Fallen Hero (Andy, Jed, and Diana)
The Search *(An Outsider Series Short)*
The Awakening (Andy and Laura)
Secrets (Jed and Diana)
Runaway (Andy and Laura)
Overdue *(An Outsider Series Short)*
The Unexpected Storm (Neil and Candy)
The Wedding (Neil and Candy)

The Friessens: A New Beginning

The Deadline (Andy and Laura)
The Price to Love (Neil and Candy)
A Different Kind of Love (Brad and Emily)
A Vow of Love, A Friessen Family Christmas

The Friessens

The Reunion
The Bloodline (Andy & Laura)
The Promise (Diana & Jed)
The Business Plan (Neil & Candy)
The Decision (Brad & Emily)
First Love (Katy)
Family First
Leave the Light On
In the Moment
In the Family

In the Silence
In the Charm
Unexpected Consequences
It Was Always You
The First Time I Saw You
Welcome to My Arms
Welcome to Boston
I'll Always Love You
Ground Rules
A Reason to Breathe
You Are My Everything
Anything For You
The Homecoming
Stay Away From My Daughter
The Bad Boy
A Place of Our Own
The Visitor
All About Devon
Long Past Dawn
How to Heal a Heart
Keep Me In Your Heart

The O'Connells
The Neighbor
The Third Call
The Secret Husband
The Quiet Day
The Commitment
The Missing Father
The Hometown Hero
Justice
The Family Secret
The Fallen O'Connell
The Return of the O'Connells

And The She Was Gone
The Stalker
The O'Connell Family Christmas
The Girl Next Door
Broken Promises
The Gatekeeper
The Hunted

The McCabe Brothers
Don't Stop Me (Vic)
Don't Catch Me (Chase)
Don't Run From Me (Aaron)
Don't Hide From Me (Luc)
Don't Leave Me (Claudia)
Out of Time

A Billy Jo McCabe Mystery
Nothing As it Seems
Hiding in Plain Sight
The Cold Case
The Trap
Above the Law
The Stranger at the Door
The Children
The Last Stand
The Charity
The Sacrifice

The Street Fighter
Finding Home

The Wilde Brothers
The One (Joe and Margaret)
The Honeymoon, A Wilde Brothers Short

Friendly Fire (Logan and Julia)
Not Quite Married, A Wilde Brothers Short
A Matter of Trust (Ben and Carrie)
The Reckoning, A Wilde Brothers Christmas
Traded (Jake)
Unforgiven (Samuel)
The Holiday Bride

Married in Montana
His Promise
Love's Promise
A Promise of Forever

The Parker Sisters
Thrill of the Chase
The Dating Game
Play Hard to Get
What We Can't Have
Go Your Own Way
A June Wedding

Kate & Walker
One Night
Edge of Night
Last Night

Walk the Right Road Series
The Choice
Lost and Found
Merkaba
Bounty
Blown Away: The Final Chapter
He Came Back

The Saved Series

Saved

Vanished

Captured

Single Titles

Loving Christine

www.ingramcontent.com/pod-product-compliance
Lightning Source LLC
Chambersburg PA
CBHW030939210726
48290CB00007B/2248
9781998775347